THRAXAS
and the
WARRIOR MONKS

Look out for these other Thraxas adventures
from Martin Scott

THRAXAS
THRAXAS AT THE RACES

THRAXAS
and the
WARRIOR
MONKS

Martin Scott

ORBIT

An *Orbit* Book

First published in Great Britain by Orbit 1999

Copyright © Martin Scott 1999

The moral right of the author has been asserted.

A CIP catalogue record for this book
is available from the British Library.

ISBN 1 85723 731 5

Typeset by Solidus (Bristol) Ltd, Bristol
Printed and bound in Great Britain by
Mackays of Chatham plc, Chatham, Kent

Orbit
A Division of
Little, Brown and Company (UK)
Brettenham House
Lancaster Place
London WC2E 7EN

CHAPTER
ONE

Makri steps into the Avenging Axe, her sword at her hip and her philosophy notes in her hand. Perspiration runs down her neck.

'It's hotter than Orcish hell out there,' she complains.

I grunt in agreement. I don't have the energy to do much more. It's hotter than Orcish hell in here too. It's as much as I can do to get my beer up to my mouth.

Makri is due to start her shift as barmaid. She takes off the man's tunic she wears outdoors and tosses it behind the bar, then sluices some water from the pitcher over her face and neck. It runs down over her tiny chainmail bikini, a garment that displays almost all of her physique and guarantees a healthy flow of tips from the dockers, sailors, Barbarian mercenaries and other low-life who drink in this tavern.

Makri lives in a small room upstairs. I also live here, in a couple of rooms further down the corridor. My name is Thraxas, and when the heat isn't so fierce that it's impossible to move, I work for a living as a Private Investigator.

Finest Sorcerous Investigator in the City of Turai says the sign on my outside door. Okay, I admit my sorcerous powers are now limited and diminishing all the time, but while I might not be able to perform like a high-class Palace Sorcerer I still know a spell or two. I still have the finely tuned senses you develop when you study magic. And I'm a determined man when I'm on a case. So I figure the sign is accurate enough.

I don't bother mentioning that I charge cheap rates. Everyone knows that already. Since I lost my job at the Palace I wouldn't say my life has worked out especially well.

I raise my hand limply, motioning for another beer from Gurd, ageing northern Barbarian and owner of the Avenging Axe.

'No intention of doing any work, then?' enquires Makri.

I wave my hand dismissively. 'Still going strong on the last fee.'

Six weeks ago I helped out Praetor Cicerius, and Cicerius is an important man in this city. More important than a Senator. More important than a Praetor now in fact, because he just won the election for the post of Deputy Consul, which makes him the second most senior government official after Consul Kalius, who answers only to the King.

'Yes,' I reflect, raising my beer. 'Old Cicerius was pretty generous with his money, I have to admit. As he should've been, of course. He wouldn't have won the election if I hadn't saved his reputation.'

Makri scoffs. Makri scoffs at a lot of what I say. I don't mind, usually. For one thing, she's one of the few friends I have in this filthy city. For another thing she often helps me out in my work. Not with the investigating exactly. More with the fighting. Here in Twelve Seas, the poor and crime-ridden dockland neighbourhood, people generally don't like being investigated. Most times I'm on a case I figure I'm going to have to use my sword at some point or other. Which is okay. I'm pretty good with it. But Makri is an escapee from the Orcish gladiator pits and consequently one of the most lethal swordswomen ever to walk the earth. I don't exaggerate. Makri may be only twenty-one and working as a barmaid to put a little food in her mouth and pay for her classes at the Guild College, but place her sword in one hand, her axe in the other and a row of enemies in front of her and the carnage can be quite incredible.

For seven years she fought in the Orc slave pits. As well as honing her fighting technique to near perfection, this has also given her powerful hatred of Orcs. Of course all humans hate Orcs, despite the peace treaty in force just now. But Makri's hatred is particularly fierce. Which makes the fact that she actually has some Orc blood in her veins all the more difficult for her. As well as some Elf blood. She's certainly an unusual mixture, unusual enough to take considerable abuse for it, although when she's serving drinks with her long dark hair swinging round her bronze shoulders and her small metal bikini clinging to her perfect figure, I notice the drinkers tend to forget their prejudices.

'You'll put on weight,' says Makri.

I pat my large belly in a satisfied manner.

'Let him be,' says Gurd, grinning, as he pulls me another flagon. 'Thraxas doesn't like to work too hard when it's hot. I remember, back in the Orc Wars, we could never get him to do a decent day's fighting when the sun shone.'

I ignore this quite untruthful slur on my reputation. Back in the Orc Wars I fought damned hard, I can tell you. Let them mock. I deserve a rest. This time last year I was pounding the docks looking for a crazed Half-Orc who had killed eight men and damn near made me the ninth. Now, with a fat payment from Cicerius and no need to work through the rest of the burning hot summer, I'm as happy as an Elf in a tree.

'Another beer, if you please, Gurd.'

Gurd is about fifty. His face is weather-beaten and his long hair is completely grey, but his muscles are undiminished with age. They bulge as he pours the drink and passes it over the bar.

'Not tempted to get involved in this?' he asks, pointing to an article in *The Renowned and Truthful Chronicle of All the World's Events*, the thin, badly printed newssheet that specialises in reporting all of the many crimes and scandals that infest Turai. I glance at it.

'Death of a Sorcerer? No, I can live without it. He was only a minor Sorcerer, anyway.'

The *Chronicle* reports that the said Sorcerer, Thalius Green Eye, was found dead yesterday at his house in Thamlin. Poison is suspected and his household servants have been taken into custody. I remember Thalius from my days at the Palace. He was a fairly unimportant figure, more interested in casting horoscopes for young aristocrats than practising any serious magic. Which isn't to say his death will be treated lightly. Being a Sorcerer has proved to be unusually hazardous in Turai recently. Only last month Tas of the Eastern Lightning was killed along with Mirius Eagle Rider, both of them connected with the case I was working on. As Sorcerers are important to any state, particularly a small one like Turai, and as they're not in endless supply, I imagine the Guards will be working away busily on the case. Let them. If old Thalius annoyed his servants enough that they went and poisoned him, he probably got what he deserved. Degenerate, these Palace Sorcerers. Dwa addicts, most of them. Or drunks. Or both.

'Another beer, please, Gurd.'

I read the rest of the *Chronicle*. There's enough crime, but that's always the case in Turai. A Praetor's been indicted for smuggling dwa into the city, a wagonload of gold from the mines in the far north has been hijacked on its way to the King's treasury and the house of the Simnian Ambassador has been burgled.

I toss the news-sheet away. Let the Civil Guard sort it out. That's what it's paid for.

The door slams open and two unfamiliar characters walk in. Fighting men, but not the normal mercenaries we get round here on their way to join up with the King's forces. The pair of them march up to the bar and order beer. Gurd pours them a couple of tankards and they make for a table to rest from the heat.

The taller of the two, a rough-looking individual with closely cropped hair and a weatherbeaten face, halts as he passes my chair. He stares at me. I glance back casually. I recognise him. I was hoping he wouldn't recognise me. It would have made my life easier. Under the table, my hand slides automatically towards the pommel of my sword.

'Thraxas,' he says, spitting out the word.

'Have we met?' I enquire.

'You know damn well we met. I spent five years on a prison galley because of you.'

'Because of me? I didn't force you to rob that Elvish Ambassador.'

I suppose I did gather the evidence to put him away. He draws his sword with well-practised ease. His companion follows his lead and with no further discussion they leap towards me with murder in their eyes.

I'm out of my chair fast. I may be forty-three years old and have a fat belly, but I can still move when I have to. The first attacker slashes at me but I parry and riposte to send him hurtling backwards with blood spurting from his chest before whirling round to face the other assailant.

The other assailant is already lying dead. In less time than it took me to dispatch my opponent Makri has grabbed her sword from its place of concealment behind the bar, leaped into the fray and slain him.

'Thanks, Makri.'

Gurd now has his old axe in his hands and looks disappointed there is no one left for him.

'Getting slow,' he mutters.

'What was that about?' asks Makri.

'They robbed an Elvish Ambassador to the Imperial

Palace. Took his money when he was lying drunk in a brothel in Kushni. Civil Guards couldn't find them but I tracked them down. About five years back. They must have only got off the prison ship a couple of months ago.'

And now they're dead. Every time I put someone away they swear to get me, but they never usually carry out their threat. Just my bad luck this pair happened to walk into the Avenging Axe. Or their bad luck, I suppose.

I frisk the corpses from habit, with no results. Nothing linking them to any of the City's criminal gangs. Probably they were just enjoying their freedom before embarking on a life of crime again. I'd rather not have had to kill them but I don't care too much. Next time they were convicted of anything they'd have been hanged anyway. One of them has a purse hanging round his neck but it's empty. Not even a coin. Their next robbery wouldn't have been too far away.

Blood oozes over the floor.

'I'll deal with this mess,' says Makri, returning her sword to its hiding place, where it rests alongside her spare axe and a few knives and throwing stars. Makri likes weapons.

She mops up the blood then bends down to pick up the empty purse that I've discarded on the floor.

'Nice embroidery,' she says. 'I could do with a new one.'

She puts it round her neck. Seven years in the Orc gladiator pits has left Makri fairly immune to the effects of death. No qualms about putting a dead man's purse round her neck, provided it's handsomely embroidered.

Gurd and I drag the bodies outside. No one takes much notice. Corpses on the street are not an especially unusual sight in Twelve Seas. Most people are too busy scratching a living to pay them much attention.

I grab a passing child and slip him a coin to take a message to the Civil Guards informing them of what has happened. They won't be too bothered about the affair either but as I'm a licensed Investigator, it pays to keep on the right side of the law.

Back inside Makri has cleaned up the floor and is polishing the bar. I get myself another beer and sit down to rest. It's getting hotter by the minute. The bar starts to fill up. The city suffered riots recently and, as much damage remains in the streets, much construction is going on to repair it. Come lunchtime the tavern is full of workers seeking refreshment from their morning shifts on the scaffolding. It's good business for Gurd. Good business for Tanrose as well, who makes and sells the food in the tavern. She's a fine cook and I purchase one of her large venison pies for lunch. With plenty of money left after my last case I've sworn to survive the rest of the burning hot summer without working. This morning's fighting came too close to work for my liking.

'What was an Elvish Ambassador doing drunk in a brothel in Kushni?' enquires Makri, later.

'Enjoying himself. His Elf Lord called him back to

the Southern Islands right afterwards in disgrace and it was all hushed up here in the city. The King never likes anything that might damage our relations with the Elves.'

I order myself another beer and wonder if I should have another venison pie. Unexpected activity tends to give me a powerful appetite.

'Everything gives you a powerful appetite,' says Makri, grinning, as she carries on cleaning the tables.

CHAPTER
TWO

After I finish my venison pie, I load up with a few of Tanrose's pastries and buy another beer to take upstairs.

'You're drinking too much,' says Tanrose.

'Needed a hobby after my wife left.'

'You took it up as a hobby long before that.'

I can't deny it.

I have two rooms at the Avenging Axe, one for sleeping and one for working. The workroom has an outside door with steps down to the street outside so clients can visit without coming up through the tavern. I'm planning to sleep the afternoon away but before I can settle down a frantic banging comes at the door. I open it and a young man rushes in, bouncing off me and ending up in the middle of the room looking scared and confused.

'They're going to hang me!' he cries. 'Don't let them do it!'

'What? Who?'

'I didn't kill him! It's a lie! Help me!'

I glare at him. My rooms are in their usual mess and he's not helping any. He's in a real state and for a long time I can't make head nor tail of what he's saying.

Eventually I have to fling him in a chair and tell him to start talking sense or get the hell out of my office. He quietens down, but keeps glancing anxiously at the door, as if he's expecting his pursuers to burst in any second.

I walk over to the door and mutter the few short sentences that make up the standard locking spell. It's a common minor spell and you don't have to be particularly skilled in magic to perform it, but the young man seems reassured.

'Now, tell me what's going on. I'm too hot to stand around guessing. Who are you, who's after you, and why?'

'The Guards! They say I killed Drantaax!'

'Drantaax? The sculptor?'

He nods.

Drantaax is a well-known man in Turai. Best sculptor in town. One of the best anywhere. Well respected for his work, even by the aristocracy, who generally look down on artisans. His statues decorate many of Turai's temples, and even the Royal Palace.

'Drantaax was murdered last night. But I didn't do it!'

'Why would anybody think you did? And who are you anyway?'

'I'm Grosex, Drantaax's apprentice. I was working with him last night. We're busy finishing off the new statue of Saint Quatinius for the Shrine. We've been working on it for days . . . but now he's dead. He was stabbed in the back.'

'Where were you at the time?'

He was next door. He came through to the

workroom and found Drantaax lying dead with a knife in his back. Then Drantaax's wife Calia arrived and starting screaming.

'Calia called the Guard. All the time she was shouting at me, saying I'd stabbed him. But I didn't.'

He hangs his head. He's running on nervous energy and it's making him ill. I offer him a thazis stick. Thazis, a mild narcotic, is still illegal but everyone uses it – well, everyone in Twelve Seas anyway. As he inhales the smoke his features relax.

I demand more details. I frown when I learn that instead of waiting for the Guards he fled the scene. And he mentions the interesting fact that the knife sticking in Drantaax belonged to him. I raise an eyebrow. It's not exactly hard to understand why everyone might think he did it. He's spent the night hiding in alleyways, wondering what to do, and now he's here, trying to hire a detective who, frankly, is not too keen to be hired. I'm still too hot, I don't need the work, and for all I know he's guilty as hell.

He looks pathetic. Even though I'm hardened to most things in Turai, I almost feel sorry for him.

There's more banging on my door.

'Open up, it's the Guard.'

I recognise the voice. It's Tholius. As Prefect of Twelve Seas he's in charge of the Civil Guard in the area. Naturally enough he despises me. Guards don't like Private Investigators. It's odd that the Prefect himself is here. Normally he'd consider himself too important to get out on the streets and do police work.

I ignore the banging. It doesn't go away.

'Thraxas, open up. I know Grosex is in there.'

'No one here but me.'

'That's not what our Sorcerer says.'

I glance at Grosex. If the Guards reckon the case is important enough to track him with an official Sorcerer he's certainly in bad trouble.

I'm still deciding what to do when the matter is taken out of my hands. The door groans as the Prefect orders his men to break it down. It's not much of a door, and my locking spell is not much of a spell. To my extreme annoyance it caves in under the weight of heavy Guards' boots and they flood in to my rooms.

I explode with anger. 'What the hell do you think you're doing, smashing your way into my rooms? You can't break your way in here without a warrant!'

Prefect Tholius waves a warrant in my face and brushes past me. It's probably not filled in properly, but I don't bother arguing.

'One false move out of him – arrest him,' he orders his Guards.

He confronts young Grosex. The apprentice, worn out from worry and still dressed in his dust-covered work tunic, cowers before the yellow-edged official toga of the Prefect.

'You're in serious trouble,' rasps Tholius, grabbing Grosex roughly by his tunic. 'Why did you kill the sculptor?'

The apprentice hopelessly protests his innocence. Prefect Tholius sneers, then shoves him into the waiting arms of two large Guards.

'Take him away. If he tries to run, kill him. And as

for you, Thraxas . . .' He turns on me. 'Don't dare interfere with the law again. If I so much as hear a rumour you're involved in this case I'll be down on you like a bad spell.'

He turns to go, but halts at the ruined door.

'Feel free to file a claim for compensation from the authorities,' he says, laughing. Any such claim would have to go to the Prefect for authorisation.

After bagging his suspect and insulting me the Prefect is as happy as an Elf in a tree and walks off smiling. The Guards depart, dragging young Grosex with them. My last sight of him, he's being hauled down the stairs into a covered Guard wagon, still pathetically protesting his innocence.

I shut what's left of my door. I finish the rest of my beer, then head downstairs to see Makri.

'I'm working,' I tell her. 'Got a case.'

'Since when?'

'Since Prefect Tholius smashed down my door and dragged a client of mine away to prison. I didn't want to work, but I am now angrier than a wounded dragon and I will consequently move heaven, earth and the three moons in order to demonstrate to Tholius that I am not a man to be treated in this way. I'm off to investigate. See you later.'

I march out into Quintessence Street with my sword at my hip and grim feelings in my heart. When I was Senior Investigator at the Palace people used to treat me with respect. I've fallen a long way since then but I'm damned if I'm going to let some petty tyrant like Prefect Tholius walk all over me.

It's hotter than Orcish hell out here and the stink of fish from the harbour market hangs thick in the air. I have to pick my way over mounds of rubble around the site of some new construction where the old houses were destroyed in the riots. In their place a contractor is raising new blocks of tenements on either side of the narrow street. Four storeys is the legal maximum in Turai but they'll probably go higher. More profit for the builders and slum landlords. And Tholius. Prefects oversee the building in their area and Tholius rakes in a fair amount in bribes by turning a blind eye to things. Perks of his job. Most Prefects are the same. So are the Praetors. Corruption goes a long way up in this city. The building contractors themselves are in league with the Brotherhood, the criminal organisation that runs the south of the city. They have to be. You can't do much around here unless the Brotherhood is involved.

There are two Civil Guard stations in Turai. The main one nearby is commanded by Prefect Tholius and a smaller one down by the docks is under the charge of Captain Rallee. I know him well, but he resolutely refuses to allow any of his men to pass on any information to me. I also have a contact at the main station, Guardsman Jevox, who's not above passing me the odd fragment of information since I got his father off a rap a few years back, but I can't risk running into the Prefect again so soon. Tholius doesn't spend too much time here – most often he's lounging around in some brothel or bar in Kushni, spending the gurans he's extorted – but he might well still be around, questioning poor Grosex.

The matter is decided when Guardsman Jevox comes out of the station and makes a frantic warning face as he sees me. I step out of sight around the corner. Peering round, I catch sight of Tholius and two Guards leading Grosex in handcuffs into a covered wagon. They drive off, with Jevox forming part of the horse escort. My official enquiries will have to wait. Which brings me swiftly to some unofficial ones. I walk on, ignoring the beggars. There's too many of them to do anything else.

At the end of Quintessence Street I turn into Tranquillity Lane, a miserable and filthy little alleyway full of prostitutes and dwa addicts. The prostitutes ignore me. The dwa addicts hold out their hands, begging. Since dwa, a powerful drug, swept the city a few years back there are more and more addicts loitering on the streets, making Twelve Seas a dangerous place to walk around after dark – or at any time, really.

Some way along Tranquillity Lane is the Mermaid, a tavern so disreputable that no one with any sense, breeding or dignity would go within a mile of the place. I seem to end up here often. Kerk, an informer of mine, can usually be found here, slumped at a table or lying on the floor if the dwa has got to him. Kerk deals dwa to support his habit and comes across much useful information, which he sells, also to support his habit.

I find him outside the tavern, lying on the sun-baked earth. There's an empty flagon of ale by his feet and the air around him has the distinctive aroma of burning dwa.

I nudge him awake with my foot. He stares up at me with his large eyes, eyes that suggest that somewhere along the line there's Elvish blood in his family, which wouldn't be all that strange. Elves visiting the cities of men are not above romantic liaisons with the prostitutes that work here. The Southern Islands of the Elves are paradise on earth, but they're short on prostitution. I guess the young Elves have to satisfy their urges somehow.

'What do you want?' mumbles Kerk.

'You know anything about Drantaax?'

He holds out his hand automatically. I drop a small coin into his palm, a tenth of a guran.

'Sculptor. Got killed last night.'

'You know anything else?'

'Stabbed by his apprentice. So they say.'

By the expression in his eyes I guess he knows a little more. I drop another coin into his palm.

'The apprentice was sleeping with his wife.'

'Is that rumoured or certified fact?'

'Rumour. But a strong one.'

The sun beats down. In the narrow confines of Tranquillity Lane it is close to unbearable. I've marched over deserts that were cooler than this. Kerk knows nothing else but says he'll keep his ear to the ground. I give him another coin and he hauls himself to his feet, now having sufficient money to buy some dwa.

I turn and leave. Not much news from Kerk, but interesting enough. Always makes things more interesting when the apprentice is sleeping with the master's wife. Unfortunately it also makes it more likely that Grosex did kill him, which is something I don't want to be true, though I've no real reason for holding him to be innocent, apart from a vague feeling that he wasn't lying. And my intense dislike of Prefect Tholius.

Stals, the small black birds that infest the city, sit brooding in the heat along the walls of the alley. They rise in the air, squawking, as they are disturbed by a stone tossed by a youth wearing the yellow bandanna which marks him out as a member of the Koolu Kings, the local youth gang. He picks up another stone.

'Toss that in my direction, kid, and I'll ram it down your throat then rot your guts with a spell.'

He backs off. Being an Investigator, I'm not exactly popular with the Koolu Kings, but they know not to mess with me. When I'm on a case on a hot day like this I'm not a man to laugh and joke with.

He sneers as I walk past. I sneer back. Kids. They used to steal fruit from the market till dwa swept the city. Now they rob people at knifepoint to buy drugs. Turai is going to hell, and quickly. If the population doesn't just riot, steal and drug its way to extinction then King Lamachus of Nioj will sweep down from the north and wipe us off the face off the earth. All he needs is an excuse, and not a particularly good one at that.

Having at least made a little progress I decide to call back in at the Avenging Axe before heading off to see what I can find out at Drantaax's studio. If I've got a whole day's investigating in front of me I need a beer, and maybe some food. It's also in my mind that I should check a few spells in my books. I freely admit that I'm not much of a Sorcerer these days – I even find it too tiring to carry the standard protection spell around in my head – but I am still able to work a trick or two. It annoyed the hell out of me that Prefect Tholius was able to waltz in and arrest Grosex right under my nose. Very bad for my reputation, if my clients get dragged away like that.

I'm preoccupied with dodging the rubble in the street outside so it takes me a second or two to focus on the figure that greets me as I walk into the tavern. I'm used to fairly strange spectacles on the streets of Turai: chanting pilgrims, hulking northern Barbarians, the occasional green-clad Elf. Closer to home, Makri herself is an exotic sight with her red-bronze skin bulging out of her chainmail bikini. Furthermore she has recently had her nose pierced with a ring, a very unusual sight in this city, and one that I strongly disapprove of. It was done for her by Palax and Kaby, a pair of travelling buskers and musicians who are an even more colourful young pair, with their hair dyed bright colours, their clothes even brighter and multiple facial piercings to boot. But it doesn't prepare me for the sight of a young woman in bare feet – a ridiculously dangerous thing to do given the state of the streets – wearing a long skirt dyed with the signs of the zodiac and a garland of flowers woven into her hair.

I blink stupidly as she stands in front of me. I can't think of any reason she would not be wearing shoes.

'Hey, Thraxas,' says Makri, appearing with a tray.

'This is Dandelion. She wants to hire you.'

Before I have time to object that no one can possibly be called Dandelion she takes my hand, stares deeply into my eyes and pronounces that's she's sure she's come to the right man.

'I can tell you have a sympathetic soul.'

Makri is sniggering somewhere in the background.

'You want to hire me?'

'Yes. On behalf of the dolphins.'

'The dolphins?'

'The dolphins that live in the bay.'

'The ones that can talk to humans,' chips in Makri.

I grunt. It's said that the dolphins can talk. Personally, I find it hard to believe.

'They sing as well,' adds Dandelion, brightly.

I'm struggling to keep my temper under control.

'I'm a busy man. Is there any point in this wildlife lecture?'

'Why, yes. The dolphins are in terrible trouble. Someone has stolen their healing stone. They want to hire you to get it back.'

'Their healing stone?'

'That's right. It's very precious to them. It fell from the sky.'

Dandelion smiles sweetly. I abandon all efforts to keep my temper.

'Will you move out the way, please? I'm a busy man and I'm working on a case. A real case. A murder. I've got no time to stand here and listen to some fool with flowers in her hair ramble on about dolphins and a healing stone that fell from the sky. Now, excuse me.'

I brush my way past. Dandelion leaps in front of me.
'But you must help them!'
'Find another Investigator.'
'The dolphins want you. They've agreed that you're in tune with them at a very deep level.'

It's as much as I can do to avoid slapping her. Makri, I note, is finding the whole thing highly amusing. Fine. Let her go and help the dolphins. I have a murder to investigate. I march up the stairs, not even stopping for my beer. I need something stronger and hunt out a bottle of klee, the spirit distilled locally in the hills outside the city. After my recent successes I've bought a better brand than I could normally afford. It still burns my throat as it goes down. I shake my head, and take another drink. Talking dolphins indeed. I've enough problems with Orcs, Elves and Humans. The fish can look after themselves.

CHAPTER
THREE

After the distraction of the ridiculous Dandelion and her dolphin ramblings I return to the real world and head off towards Drantaax's workshop. I've already walked more than enough in this heat so I hire a landus and sit back and let the small horse-drawn carriage take me out of Twelve Seas and north into Pashish. Pashish is a calmer area than Twelve Seas, home to the poor but respectable workers and their families who keep this city going. There isn't much wealth here but the streets are a little wider and less sordid than those close to the harbour. My friend Astrath Triple Moon, the Sorcerer, lives close by and I'll probably call in on him later.

While riding I'm thinking about two things. One, who killed Drantaax? Two, who is going to pay me to find out? As the heat of my anger from Tholius's invasion of my rooms fades a little, it strikes me that I have plunged into a case without receiving a fee, which is unusual for me. I don't do this for fun. It's my living. Technically I don't even have a client. Grosex was apprehended before he had time to hire me. The worrying thought occurs that being a young apprentice he might not have any money. He might have spent all his meagre wages on presents for the sculptor's wife.

I'll have to hope for the best. Just because I'm not actually desperate for money doesn't mean that I've suddenly come over all charitable. The way my life goes these days, I'll be poor again soon enough. Probably right after the next chariot race.

The landus is halted at a corner by a passing group of chanting pilgrims on their way to visit the shrine of Saint Quatinius over on the west side of the city. I reach out and grab a news-sheet from a vendor. *The Renowned and Truthful Chronicle of All the World's Events* is always keen to report lurid goings-on and the death of the sculptor is a major story. Murder is common in this city, but Drantaax was well enough known for it to be big news. A number of different artists work in Turai, attracted by the wealth that still circulates among our decadent upper classes, but none was as renowned as Drantaax.

The news-sheet says that the statue he was working on, a life-size figure of Saint Quatinius on horseback, was partly funded by the True Church in Nioj. It describes the crime without much detail, then goes on to report that the statue is missing. I presume this must be a misprint. We have many smart criminals in Turai but I can't imagine anyone making off unnoticed with a life-size bronze statue of a man on horseback. God knows what it would weigh. The Niojan angle is bad news though. Nioj is a fundamentalist state. Their King is also their Chief Pontifex and a religious fanatic to boot, so this will give them plenty of reason to be annoyed with Turai.

Drantaax's house is located at the far end of Pash-ish, where things start to get a little more comfortable. The streets are clean and the pavement is in good repair. I dismount a block away, pay the driver, and walk up. The house and workshop are guarded outside by two Civil Guards. When I inform them I'm here on business they stare at me stony-faced and refuse to budge.

'That's all we need,' comes a voice from behind me. 'Thraxas poking his fat belly into Guard matters.'

I turn round. 'Hello, Captain Rallee. Glad to see you're on the case.'

'Well, it's not mutual. What do you want?'

Captain Rallee and I go back a long way. We fought together in the Orc Wars. Along with Gurd, we had some hair-raising times, which I still regale an audi-ence with while drinking in the Avenging Axe. After the war, when I was Senior Investigator at the Palace, Captain Rallee also spent a lot of time there before falling out of favour with Deputy Consul Rittius and finding himself once more pounding the streets. His Guard station down at the harbour is in one of the toughest patches in town, which is saying something. Rallee doesn't mind that's it's rough – he's not the sort of man to flinch from his duty – but he feels a man of his experience should have moved on to something better by now.

Though we were once fairly close and were also both bounced out of the Palace by Rittius, we've grown apart in the past few years. I'm freelance now, and Rallee's a Guard, and these two breeds are never comfortable with each other. The Captain has done me the odd favour and he knows I'm no fool, but finding him on the case is no guarantee of any inside help.

'How's life in the Civil Guard?'

'Better than rowing a slave galley. There again, with you around, maybe not.'

I tell him he's looking well, which is true. He carries his age better than I do. His hair hangs down his back in a thick pony tail, as does mine, but his is blond and shining. So is his moustache. Mine is starting to show signs of grey. I imagine the ladies still like him.

The Captain brushes aside my compliment. 'You working on this or just poking your nose in for the sake of it?'

'Just earning a living, Captain. Grosex hired me before Tholius got to him.'

'The apprentice? He hired you? What with?'

'He paid my standard retainer,' I lie.

The Captain snorts and tells me it's well known that Grosex didn't have a penny to his name, never mind a thirty-guran retainer to hire an Investigator.

'So is it true he was having an affair with Drantaax's wife?'

The Captain shrugs. 'So they say. Something was making Calia happy anyway, according to the servants.'

'Where is he now?'

'Prison. And you're not going to see him. Tholius has him locked up tight and he's not going to risk any

of his credit for a quick arrest by letting you interfere.
This is bad, Thraxas. The True Church in Turai spent a
long time persuading the Niojan Church to help fund
the statue. They were going to invite some Niojan
clerics down for the inauguration ceremony. Meant to
help us get along better I guess. Now the sculptor's
dead and the statue's gone. King Lamachus won't like
that at all.'

'Where's the wife? I need to speak to her.'

'You can't.'

I'm getting annoyed at this. 'What's eating you,
Captain? Since when is an Investigator forbidden to
talk to a witness?'

'No one's forbidding anything. You can't speak to
her because she's missing. Took a hike before we got
here.'

According to the Captain, Calia sent a servant to alert
the Guards after Drantaax's body was found. When they
arrived she'd gone.

'No one saw her leave. Calia slipped off amid the
confusion. So now we have one dead sculptor, one
missing wife and one missing statue.'

'The statue is really gone? How could anyone move
it?'

The Captain shrugs. 'No idea. But it's gone all right.
All two tons of it.'

'Tholius traced Grosex to my place with a Sorcerer.
Can't the Sorcerer find the statue?'

'Apparently not. And no, before you ask, no traces
of sorcery were found at the scene. Our men went over
the whole place without finding the slightest trace of

anything magical. How the statue managed to disappear is a mystery. The servants swear that Drantaax was working on the statue that morning. Drantaax's wife found the body right after he was killed, so there was no time for the statue to disappear. But it did.'

'Why is Tholius so sure Grosex did it?'

'Grosex's knife was sticking in the corpse.'

'So? That doesn't mean anything. Anyone could have used his knife.'

'Maybe. We'll see what our Sorcerer says when he examines the weapon, but I figure he'll find Grosex's aura on it all right. Now, I'm busy. If you don't mind I'll get on with my work.'

'I need to see inside.'

'Go to hell.'

Captain Rallee used to be liaison officer between the Abode of Justice, which controls the Civil Guard, and Palace Security. A nice comfy job, though after many years at the sharp end of crime in Turai he deserved it. Now he's back pounding the streets and he doesn't like it at all. He is rarely in the best of moods.

'Come on, what's the matter? I have a right to go in.'

'"What's the matter?" What's the matter is I have Prefect Tholius on my tail looking for this one to be wrapped up quickly so we can keep Nioj and the True Church happy and I already have Consul Kalius on my tail about the King's hijacked gold shipment, as well as a million other things, from pilgrims being robbed at the shrine to eight dwa-related killings in Kushni in the past two days. Is that enough for you?'

I make sympathetic noises but point out that as the

official representative of Grosex I have a legal right to examine the scene of the crime. The Captain ponders for a while. He doesn't want me inside but, to be fair to him, he's not a man to flout the law.

'Take a look, then. If Tholius appears and chucks you in jail, don't come crying to me.'

At this moment, as we are about to enter the house, the call for afternoon prayers rings out from the many towers scattered throughout the city and we are all obliged to kneel with our heads bowed to the ground. There's no avoiding this in Turai. Three times a day we have official prayers and anyone not found kneeling is in trouble with the authorities. So I kneel and pray next to Captain Rallee and the two Guards, which is funny in a way, though often while working I've found myself obliged to pray in far stranger company. I've even found myself fighting an opponent when the call rang out, and been obliged to kneel down beside him, pray, then stand up again and kill him. At least he went to meet his maker well prepared.

The heat is intense and I have to struggle to stay awake. When the call for the end of prayers rings out I drag myself wearily to my feet.

'You're getting slow, Thraxas,' says Captain Rallee. 'It's time you got off the streets. Try opening a tavern.'

'I'd drink myself out of business.'

We enter the house, and I quickly get down to examining the scene of the crime under the watchful eye of a Guard who's assigned to follow me and make sure I don't do anything I shouldn't.

Drantaax's house is a standard enough building, a

little grander than most but nothing special. If it wasn't for the exquisite statues decorating the rooms, garden and central courtyard it could be the dwelling place of any moderately prosperous businessman. The statues are beautiful though. Even an untrained eye such as mine can tell at a glance that they are of a higher quality than most things you find around our cities' temples and libraries.

Drantaax's large workshop is joined on to the back of the house but there isn't much to see at the scene of the crime, other than a faint blood stain where the body was and a large empty space where the statue ought to be. I concentrate to see if I can detect the aura of magic, but I can't. I'm pretty sure none has been used here in the past few days. According to Captain Rallee the statue was definitely here yesterday. It was seen by the Pontifex from the True Church, sent to see how it was progressing.

The statue was a bronze cast. Drantaax carves it out of plaster, then sends it to a foundry who casts it for him and ships it back in six pieces. After that the sculptor puts the pieces together, files it down, makes any final adjustments, and there you are, one bronze statue. Statues of that kind are hollow inside but Drantaax had finished assembling it so it must have weighed a couple of tons, saint, horse and plinth.

And now it's gone. Vanished. No one saw a thing. When the statue was finished it would have taken six men with lifting gear and a specially strengthened cart to move it out. I study the winches at the end of the workshop designed for moving the heavy artifices.

A cumbersome process, I'm sure. Not something you could do in a hurry. But someone did shift it, and no one saw a thing. None of the neighbours or any by-stander the Guard has been able to trace saw anything unusual in or around the house. A beggar sits across the street every day and he swears that no wagon left the yard on the day of the murder.

'It can't just have disappeared.'

Captain Rallee informs me dryly that he'd already worked that out for himself.

'And Old Hasius the Brilliant says no sorcery was involved? Very strange.'

Other statues are in the workshop, some still being worked on, others now complete. Fine statues, valu-able, I imagine, to a collector. All of them are smaller, some of them only busts that one man could carry. So why did the thief choose to take such a massive thing with him instead? It would be impossible to sell, even in Turai, favoured home of the crooked merchant.

Outside the workshop is a flowerbed where a small sculptured Wood Nymph reclines in a bed of red flowers. The flowers have lasted well in the fierce summer heat, but are now starting to wilt. Petals cover the path, making a small red patch. With a tiny piece of yellow in the middle. I bend down for a closer look. There are a few yellow petals in among the red. I glance at the flowerbed again. None of the flowers there are yellow. Strange. Maybe there were only a few yellow petals and they all fell off? Maybe not. I pick up the yellow petals and place them in the small pouch at my hip I carry for such occasions.

I look around a short while more without learning anything. Captain Rallee tells me he has no leads on the whereabouts of Drantaax's wife. If he knows anything, he isn't saying. He has all three of Drantaax's servants locked up for questioning and there doesn't seem any immediate prospect of me being able to see them. I figure it's time to leave.

I need to see Grosex quickly but as I'm close to the home of Astrath Triple Moon I decide to call in there first. Astrath is a Sorcerer, and a good one, and he might be able to help.

While walking down the street it strikes me that I'm being followed. I can always tell, have an instinct for it. It's part of the sensitivity I developed as a young Sorcerer's Apprentice and it served me well when I was a mercenary. The feeling is still there when I reach Astrath's house. As I ring his bell I quickly look round, but no one is in sight.

A servant leads me into the house which is a great deal smaller than you would expect for the home of a powerful Sorcerer like Astrath Triple Moon. Like me, he's come down in the world. Astrath found himself in trouble a couple of years ago and is lucky to still be in the city at all. He was employed as official Sorcerer at the Stadium Superbius, with responsibility for seeing that all the fights and chariot races were above board and not influenced by magic.

The citizens of Turai are very sensitive about this – no one wants to bet on a chariot and then find it's been hexed – so the resident Sorcerer has an important job. After a series of strange results the word went around that Astrath was taking bribes to turn a blind eye to sorcerous interference. He was in grave danger of a lengthy prison sentence or possibly a public lynching till I dug around a little and cleared his name – well, not exactly cleared his name, as he was in fact guilty as hell, but I muddied the water enough that no proof could be brought to court. Astrath consequently managed to avoid expulsion from the Sorcerers Guild but he was compelled to quit his job. The scandal forced him out of his lavish villa in Thamlin and landed him here in Pashish, ministering to the needs of the poor.

I often ask him for advice. He might have a weakness for taking bribes but he's sharp as an Elf's ear on all things sorcerous. He's also a generous man with his food and drink, and generally pleased to see me. None of his old buddies in the Sorcerers Guild would come within a mile of him these days, which leaves him short of intelligent conversation.

As I walk in he's already instructing a servant to bring in wine and fruit. His small front room is crammed full of books, potions and other magical paraphernalia and he has to brush several rolls of paper away to make space for the decanter.

'How's life?' I ask.

'Better than rowing a slave galley, but not much. If I have to draw up another horoscope for the local fishwife I swear I'll poison her next catch. Gets me down, Thraxas. The woman has fourteen children and she wants to know everything the future holds for each one of them. How the hell am I meant to know if her seventh daughter is going to make a good marriage?'

He sighs, and pours some wine. We chat for a while about affairs in the city, speculating whether things might improve now Cicerius is Deputy Consul, and if war with Nioj or Mattesh is likely.

'You hear about Drantaax?'

Astrath has. 'Fine sculptor. As soon as I heard about it I checked the conjunctions to see if I could learn anything, but they're way off.'

Powerful Sorcerers such as Astrath Triple Moon can sometimes look back in time. Fortunately for the criminals of Turai, it's a very difficult feat, and completely impossible if the three moons were in the wrong phases when compared with their current position in the sky. Occasionally the Sorcerers at the Abode of Justice have pulled off a spectacular coup in difficult criminal cases by peering through time and identifying precisely who was there and what happened, but it's a very rare occurrence. Most often the Guards have to pound the streets asking questions, the same as me.

I fill him in on what I know of the case and ask him about the statue. 'Any ideas how it could have been moved?'

He strokes his beard. Beards are uncommon in Turai but they're favoured by Sorcerers and a few other guilds, like the Tutors and the Storytellers for instance.

'No sign of magic at all?'

'None. Guards didn't find any and I'd swear nobody had uttered a spell there recently. I might not have made it much past Apprentice Sorcerer but in my line of work you learn to recognise it.'

'A good Sorcerer might be able to hide it, Thraxas. Which Guard Sorcerer checked the place out?'

'Old Hasius the Brilliant.'

'Old Hasius himself, eh? Must be important if the Guard got him down from the Abode of Justice. Well, that changes things. No Sorcerer could hide all traces of his aura or his spells from Old Hasius. He's a cranky old soul, but he knows his magic. The statue must have been carried out manually.'

'Impossible. There wasn't time. It was there in the morning. Various people will swear to it. And Drantaax's workshop is on the main street in Pashish. There is no way that someone wouldn't have seen it being removed on a wagon. It would have taken six men and an hour to load it. Major operation. But no one saw a thing. The statue just vanished. I know that Old Hasius the Brilliant's been scanning the city for it, but he can't find a thing.'

Astrath agrees that the whole thing is very odd but can't offer any suggestions. 'When it comes right down to it, Thraxas, does it matter to you what happened to the statue? If you just want to clear Grosex of the murder, I mean.'

'Good point, Astrath. It might not matter at all if I can find some other angle. But the Prefect has him locked up tight and it's hard to get a lead. I guess if I knew where the statue was I'd probably find out what was behind it all. And it might produce some results for the Guard Sorcerers once they had a good look at the aura.'

He agrees to scan the city himself to see if he can come up with anything.

Before I go I ask him if he has any suggestions for preventing a repeat of this morning's debacle where Tholius walked in and took Grosex away.

'An invisibility spell?' he suggests. 'Make your client unseeable by the authorities.'

'Way beyond me, I'm afraid. I could never get it to work. My powers don't rise much above the sleep spell for knocking out opponents these days.'

'Hmm.'

He takes his grimoire off a shelf and hunts through the index. 'How about this? Temporary bafflement. Simple little spell. Makes anyone searching your rooms very confused indeed. Not foolproof, of course, if you're up against anyone strong-willed enough, but it should be enough of a distraction to let you conceal anyone from nosy Civil Guards.'

That sounds like it might work. I thank him, finish up my wine and take my leave. After the coolness of Astrath's house the evening streets are still unbearably hot, and walking home I am followed again. I don't try to shake them, preferring instead to discover their identity, but the culprit is tricky and I fail to get a glimpse of him.

Back at the Avenging Axe Makri has finished her shift and is about to disappear up to her room to study mathematics, which is part of her course at the Guild College. It is Makri's ambition to attend the Imperial University. This is impossible as the Imperial University does not admit women students. It only admits the sons of Senators or the richest of our merchants, and it is certainly not likely to accept anyone with Orc blood in her veins. Despite this, Makri refuses to be deterred.

'The Guild College didn't want to admit me either,' she points out. 'And look how well I'm doing there.'

'Last week you had a fight with *eight* of your fellow students.'

'They insulted my ears.'

One consequence of Makri's unusual parentage is that her ears are rather pointed, though as her hair is so long and thick, they're usually hidden from view.

'So? I've insulted your ears plenty of times.'

'You're a drunken oaf who doesn't know any better,' counters Makri. 'Students ought to be polite. Anyway, I wouldn't really call it a fight. Most of them just ran away. And I passed the philosophy exam right afterwards.'

I notice that Makri has secreted a few thazis sticks from behind the bar among her sheaf of papers. I take one from her as we walk upstairs.

'Better not let Gurd catch you stealing his thazis.'

'He should pay me better. Why wouldn't you help the dolphins?'

'Help the dolphins? You mean work for Dandelion? You must be joking. I'm an Investigator on a murder case. I haven't the time to traipse round after some social misfit with flowers in her hair listening to some so-called talking dolphins bleat about their healing stone. The woman was obviously insane.'

Makri laughs. 'I liked her.'

'Only because you always like people that outrage me.'

'Like who?'

'Like Hanama the Assassin, that's who. Woman damn near killed me and now you go to meetings with her.'

This is a slight source of friction between myself and Makri. Makri has become involved with the Association of Gentlewomen, a group formed to advance the rights of women in Turai, which, it must be admitted, are rather limited. Can't join the guilds for one thing, apart from a few specialised ones like the Sorcerers and the Assassins. Can't join the Honourable Association of Merchants either, which puts a serious block on business opportunities and such like. Can't vote, can't sit in the Senate. Nor are they allowed in the luxurious baths and gymnasia up town. Which, I must admit, never troubled me unduly till Makri became involved with the Association and started making a big deal about it.

I'm willing to go along with her views, I guess. It's no skin off my nose. As long as I contribute a guran or two to Makri's collections, it keeps her off my back. However, as I learned to my cost recently, membership of the Association of Gentlewomen has grown alarmingly recently. It would be a great surprise to most citizens of Turai if they knew, for instance, that not only did the Association have the support of the likes of Minarixa the baker and Chiaraxi the herbal healer, but it can count on the covert support of Princess Du-Akai, third in line to the throne. The King certainly won't be

amused if he finds that out. Nor will the True Church,
who regard the Association as an abomination.

Lisutaris, Mistress of the Sky, a very powerful
Sorcerer when she can stay away from her waterpipe,
is another supporter. Strangest of all, I'm pretty sure
that Hanama, number three in the Assassins Guild, is
in there as well. The thought of Makri attending secret
meetings with these people makes me worry that
possibly some people in the city who shouldn't know
my business might occasionally be learning a few
things they oughtn't. Not that Makri would ever know-
ingly betray any of my secrets, of course, but she's
only been in the city a year and remains un-
sophisticated in the ways of civilisation. She sometimes gets cheated in the market. She finds it awkward
using cutlery. I can still lie to her and get away with it.

Makri goes off along the corridor to study. I go to
sleep.

CHAPTER
FOUR

Next day I'm awake so early I almost catch morning prayers, which I haven't done for years. Despite my prompt start it's a morning of complete frustration. I take a landus up to the prison but I can't get to see Grosex. All prisoners have the legal right to see their representatives, which in this case includes me, but in Turai legal niceties aren't always respected and I'm turned away at the prison with the abrupt news that Grosex is not seeing anyone. When I protest loud and long about it an official asks me to produce evidence that I have in fact been employed by Grosex to investigate his case.

'Prefect Tholius dragged him off before he could write my authorisation.'

And that doesn't get me anywhere at all. Obviously the authorities want this wrapped up quickly without the bother of anyone constructing a reasonable defence. Grosex's trial is scheduled for next week and if this situation continues he'll certainly hang. Drantaax was valued by the city, and public opinion is baying for his killer's blood.

I curse my lack of influence with officials in this town. I have plenty of contacts in the underworld, but since getting booted out of the Palace many powerful doors have been slammed shut.

It strikes me that Cicerius, our new Deputy Consul, might be willing to go out on a limb for me after the good service I rendered him recently, but Cicerius is away on official business in Mattesh, so I am for the moment stuck.

If I can't see Grosex then I should certainly see Drantaax's wife but all my enquiries lead nowhere. No one saw her go and no one has any information as to where she might be. She has one relative in town, a brother who works in a warehouse down at the docks. He can't tell me anything and doesn't seem to care much. They never got on, apparently.

'Was she having an affair with the apprentice?' I ask him.

'Probably,' he replies, indicating it's time for me to be on my way. I hang around to be awkward but learn no more than the fact that we're bringing in a lot of wheat by ship these days.

I'm interested that Drantaax's wife Calia comes from a family of dock workers. Means she married above her class. Drantaax isn't an aristocrat but a successful sculptor ranks some way above your standard manual labourer. Everybody in Turai is conscious of such a distinction.

I visit the Guard station when Tholius is away but Guardsman Jevox doesn't know where Calia is and doesn't think the Guards have any real leads.

'It can't be that easy for a woman with no family to hide in the city. Where would she go? The servants claim she couldn't have taken any money with her. And why did she disappear?'

'Maybe she killed him so she could set up with the apprentice,' suggests Jevox.

'Well, if she did it was pretty careless to use his knife and get him hanged as a result.'

I wonder about Calia and Grosex. If they were really having an affair it seems strange that she would take to her heels and leave him in the lurch.

Jevox tells me he used to know her when she still lived down by the harbour. He remembers her as a very beautiful young woman.

'No surprise when she married a wealthy sculptor. If she'd held out she could probably have gone even higher.'

Jevox is busy. Tholius is giving his men a hard time because Senator Lodius, who leads the opposition party, the Populares, is using the recent wave of crime as a stick to beat the Traditionals with.

'Foreign Ambassadors' houses burgled!' he roars in the Senate. 'Gold stolen from the King! Honest citizens murdered in the streets! Dwa spreading like a curse through the city! And what are our representatives doing about this crisis?'

There's more more to the speech, as reported in the *Chronicle*, and it naturally makes every city official from Consul Kalius downwards uncomfortable. Senator Lodius's Populares suffered a slight reverse in the elections a few months back, but he's still a powerful man in the city, capable of causing any amount of problems if he stirs up the mob. So the Civil Guards are

all working overtime to try and solve a few out-
standing crimes and they're none too pleased about it.
I leave Jevox staring glumly at a pile of witness reports
concerning a dwa-related murder at the docks. None
of the witnesses seem to have seen anything, which is
usually the case when powerful dwa gangs commit
violence.

If I had something belonging to Calia I might be
able to work a spell to locate her but I have nothing. I
go back to the sculptor's house but it is now locked
tight and guarded and nothing I can say will get me
inside. I curse myself for not taking something when I
had the chance before. However, the Guards' Sorcerers won't make any progress in this direction either
because the moons won't be back in the right conjunction for several months. Grosex can't wait several
months.

I complain about this to Astrath Triple Moon.

'Any time I need to find someone in a hurry the
moons are in the wrong alignment. Sorcery's a bust
when it comes to solving crimes.'

'Not always. I've got you some good results in the
past.'

That's true enough. Anyway, it's just as well sorcery can't solve all the crime in the city, otherwise I'd
be out of a job.

Astrath scans the city for the statue, without success. Which seems to make it certain that it's gone far
away, but how remains a mystery. Back in the Avenging Axe I complain about my lack of progress to
Makri.

'The only thing that's happening is I'm getting followed.'

'Followed? Who by?'

'I don't know. Haven't caught so much as a glimpse. But I can feel it.'

'Have you tried the kuriya?'

I shake my head. Kuriya, a dark and mysterious liquid, will sometimes yield up a picture in reply to a question, provided the enquirer has been trained in the process. It's something I can still do with reasonable results on occasion, though it completely drains me these days. However, it doesn't always work and the liquid, imported from the far west, is hideously expensive, so I'll only really be able to try it once. I'd rather get information about Grosex than whoever is tailing me. I'll look after them in person when they show their faces.

I finish my lunchtime ale. I can't see Grosex and I can't find any witnesses to what went on and I need to know. I turn my thoughts back to Drantaax's wife Calia. Perhaps the kuriya might give me a hint. Worth trying. I'm not getting anywhere without it.

It takes a long time to put myself into the required mental state. Ideally a Sorcerer should work in a peaceful environment but there is precious little quiet in Twelve Seas at the best of times, with fish vendors, dwa dealers and whores all competing to advertise their wares. Stray dogs growl and fight with each other, children play noisily in the dirt and women shout at the stallholders as they bargain for their cheapest vegetables. Apart from this uproar there's the additional noise of the builders everywhere. It's not easy to sink into a trance. I do my best.

In front of me is a saucer full of the precious black liquid. The one merchant who imports it from the far west claims that it's dragon's blood. This is not true – I've seen dragon's blood – but it gives him a reason to charge such a ridiculous price for it. Whatever its origins, it can respond to the searching mind of a skilled Sorcerer. And even me, though I never made it much past Apprentice.

I've drawn the curtains and illuminated my room with a large red candle. The shiny black liquid reflects the light. I concentrate on the flame, and think about Drantaax's wife, and where she might be.

For a while, nothing happens. Almost long enough to think that nothing will happen. I stay in my trance. Time passes. The room goes cold and I can no longer hear the noise outside. Finally a picture starts to form: a house, a large house, a white villa on a wooded hill.

I'm straining to see more clearly when my concentration is affected by a tiny nagging feeling of unease. I don't know what it is. I ignore it. It won't go away. I try and concentrate on the picture, but it's slipping. Deep in my trance, I realise that someone is in my room. A bolt of fear shoots through me, the horrible terror of being helpless in front of an enemy. I emerge from the trance with a frightened roar, leaping to my feet confused and disorientated and whirling round frantically to see who's there. My vision spins crazily for a second and then focuses sharply on two figures just yards from where I was kneeling. One of them is engaged in going through the papers on my desk while the other one keeps look-out. They're both wearing red robes. They both have shaven heads. Monk burglars?

'Who the hell are you?' I roar.

They turn and head for the door. I leap after them and grab the nearest one by the shoulder, spinning him round.

'What's going on?'

He pulls away. Still shocked by the interruption to my trance, I have even less patience than usual. I let fly with a blow that should send the monk through the wall. He blocks it. I'm surprised. I try again. He blocks it again, automatically, with no apparent effort. When I aim a third clubbing blow at his face he touches my arm and I find myself facing the other way, God knows how. Then I'm propelled across the room by a mighty slap between the shoulder blades. I bounce into the far wall and crumple on to the floor.

Makri charges in and finds me lying confused and disorientated. She rushes to the outside door, but there's no one in sight. My assailants have departed as swiftly and mysteriously as they appeared.

'Who was it?' asks Makri, helping me to my feet.

'Just two warrior monks out for a little fun,' I gasp, and sink down on the couch, exhausted from looking in the kuriya. Having to confront two warrior monks on top of that is way too much.

'What are warrior monks?'

'Monks who are also warriors. They spend half their time in prayer and meditation, and the other half learning how to fight. Excuse me, Makri, I have to lie down.'

My head swims. The blow winded me. I lie on my couch till it clears. Makri brings me a beer and I start getting back into the real world.

'Damn them. I was just starting to get a picture when they arrived.'

I strive to remember what the house in the kuriya pool was like. A villa on a wooded hill. Could be any one of a number of places up on the edges of the rich suburb of Thamlin where the land rises up towards the Palace. But it might be somewhere else – another city even.

'No, Calia couldn't have made it so far away. If she'd taken passage on a ship the Guards would have heard about it. And I don't believe she galloped off on a horse. Rallee tells me they've made a thorough check on everyone who hired out horses that day. Checked the trading caravans leaving the city as well.'

Makri wonders why the Guards are so keen. 'They're taking a lot of trouble over this, aren't they? For a run-of-the-mill murder?'

'Perhaps. But Senator Lodius is making speeches about the city going to ruin again, so the Guards are working flat out to try and prove they're not the waste of space he accuses them of being. Poor Jevox was looking forward to a week's holiday and instead he's up to his eyebrows in witness statements and is consequently about as miserable as a Niojan whore about everything. The Guards need to do a good job on Drantaax and reckon they're off to a flying start having actually arrested someone so quickly. They won't want to risk messing up the trial of his killer.'

I ought to get up to Thamlin and see if I can find that villa. Damn those monks for interrupting.

Gurd knocks and pokes his head round the door.

'Makri,' he says, 'you should be working. And Thraxas, there's someone downstairs to see you.'

'Who?'

'I think her name was Dandelion.'

'Tell her I've gone out,' I say, rising hastily. 'Important investigating. Stop looking at me like that, Makri. I am not going to look for the dolphins' healing stone that fell from the sky, and that's final. If you're so concerned, take Dandelion to one of your Association of Gentlewomen meetings. They'll sort her out.'

I grab a sword, pick up some money to buy a loaf of bread at Minarixa's bakery, and head on out.

As soon as I hit the street I know I'm being followed. I frown. I'm getting fed up with this. I jump in a landus and instruct the driver to take me to Thamlin quickly. He does his best, but, with all the construction work, the potholes in the roads and the market traffic, we move slowly and I fail to shake off my tail. I regret not dealing with this earlier.

Thamlin is a different world to the filth of Twelve Seas. Here the streets are clean and paved with pale green and yellow tiles. The luxurious villas stand behind leafy gardens and white walls manned by members of the Securitus Guild. Civil Guards patrol the streets in numbers, keeping them safe from the rabble. No one disturbs the calm. Even the stals, the small black birds which infest the city, look better fed. Anyone wandering up here to do a little begging is soon chased away so as not to disturbing the peace of our aristocracy.

I used to live here. Now I'm about as welcome as an Orc at an Elvish wedding.

Having no particularly good idea as to where to start my search I halt the landus in Truth is Beauty Lane, where the Sorcerers live, and stroll on up the gentle slope towards the wooded area adjoining the grounds of the Imperial Palace. All around me are houses similar to the one I saw in the kuriya pool. I strain to recall any distinctive features but nothing comes to mind. Just another luxurious villa where the occupants can lie around in the shade drinking wine from their own vineyards and eating fish from their private ponds. I frown. A fine piece of investigation this is turning out to be.

I notice a Guard standing outside one of the smaller villas set back from the road. No one else is in sight, no servants trimming the lawns or tending to the flower beds. It strikes me that it is very probably the house of Thalius Green Eye, the recently killed Sorcerer.

It's nothing to do with me. I should stay away. So I wander over for a look. The Guard isn't paying much attention to anything. He doesn't notice me slipping over the small wall and into the garden. I don't know why I'm doing this. Just naturally curious about Sorcerers being murdered, I guess.

The gardens are well tended but empty. Presumably all of the dead Sorcerer's servants are still in custody, answering questions about their knowledge of poisons. I walk swiftly through some tall trees till I reach a small ornamental pond at the back of the house. Unlike some of our wealthier residents, Thalius didn't keep it stocked with fish. A well-stocked fish pond is a big status symbol in Turai; an aristocratic matron couldn't ask a member of the Royal Family to dinner unless she could produce a first course from her own private source. Takes some money to maintain though.

I'm now close to the back door, painted yellow with a small statue of Saint Quatinius at each side. Yellow is regarded as the luckiest colour to paint your back door in Turai. The front one should be white. Virtually everyone falls into line on this one. Even if you're not superstitious, why tempt fate?

I'm closing in on the door when a noise inside sends me hurrying to hide behind a large bush. Another noise from behind sends me deeper into the undergrowth. I watch with interest bordering on amazement. First, the back door opens and out come three shaven-headed and red-robed monks, very quietly indeed. They glide through the portal warily, checking that they are unobserved before moving off towards the far end of the grounds. They are not unobserved, however, because from the undergrowth behind me emerge four other monks, equally shaven-headed but garbed in yellow. They immediately rush at the first group and attack them without warning.

The silence is broken as battle is joined, and a very athletic battle it is too. People talk of the fighting prowess of warrior monks but I've never seen such a demonstration myself. I watch in astonishment as kicks fly head high and crunching blows send opponents spinning great distances over the lawn, until the recipients of these blows leap athletically to their feet and run back into the fray. Most of the blows are accompanied by peculiarly intense shouts so the whole neighbourhood must surely hear what is going on.

It doesn't take long for the Civil Guard from the front of the house to arrive. When he sees the seven warring monks he wisely decides not to get involved, but blows a piercing whistle to summon help.

Hearing this, the monks disengage. They eye each other with hatred, then the uninjured help the wounded and they make off in different directions. Again, they display great agility in leaping over walls and various other obstacles between themselves and freedom.

More Civil Guards will arrive at any second. I just have time to make my escape. I ought to get as far away from here as I can. So instead I walk over to the back door and step inside. I'm a fool sometimes. My overwhelming curiosity – or nosiness – has landed me in trouble since the day I was born.

At least there's some relief in here from the baking sun outside. I sluice some water over my neck from the pitcher in the kitchen, and head on into the house. In the first room I enter – a wide, white, calm room with pastel tapestries on the walls – I meet a young woman with a knife in her hand who challenges me in a spirited manner and attempts a vicious slash at my belly before she trips over the empty bottle of klee at her feet and falls down in a drunken heap on the floor.

Another unexpected development. I frown. I'm sure

Thalius wasn't married, yet she's wearing a toga suitable for the woman of the house. Must be his daughter.

She looks up from the floor and demands to know what I'm doing here.

'Investigating the death of Thalius,' I lie.

'You're not a Guard.' She climbs unsteadily to her feet. 'Just as well. Guards won't get anywhere finding out who killed my father. Guards are as much use as a eunuch in a brothel.'

I'm surprised to hear this expression spoken in her cultured voice. She reaches for another bottle of klee on the shelf behind her. She's already had more than enough but I figure it's none of my business so I don't try and stop her. I think I can hear noises outside suggesting more Guards have arrived.

'The Guards will be here any moment. I'm an Investigator. I'll help you if you tell me about it.'

It comes out sounding sincere. It might even be sincere. I'm feeling kind of sorry for her, drunk and alone with her father freshly buried.

'What's to tell?'

'Who killed your father?'

'His dwa dealer, I suppose.'

This takes me completely by surprise. Not the fact that Thalius Green Eye took dwa – that's common enough among all classes of people and Sorcerers seem particularly prone to it. But there was no mention of any drug connection in the reports of the killing.

'I thought he was poisoned by a servant.'

She laughs, stupidly, drunkenly. 'So they say. Didn't want another drug scandal to rock the Palace. Too many already. My father wasn't poisoned. He was killed by a crossbow bolt. Couldn't pay the dwa dealer.'

There are footsteps outside as the Civil Guards enter the house.

'Hire me to find the killer,' I say, urgently, but it's too late. At the same moment as she falls unconscious to the floor the Guards enter the room led by Prefect Galwinius himself, their chief in Thamlin.

Prefect Galwinius knows me well. He dislikes me just as much as Prefect Tholius does. More, possibly. He takes one look at her outstretched body before ordering my immediate arrest and I am loaded into a wagon and carted off to jail.

It's not unusual for me to be carted off to jail in the course of an investigation but when I reflect that I have been carted off this time because of something I wasn't even investigating, I wonder if even at my stage of life it might not be too late to curb my natural inquisitiveness.

CHAPTER
FIVE

The worst thing about being in jail is the heat. And the smell. And you can't get a beer. The company's always bad as well. There's plenty wrong with being in jail.

I'm sitting in a small cell with a fellow prisoner who won't say a word and lies on his bunk looking miserable as a Niojan whore. It's actually a relief when the prayer call rings out. Gives me something to do.

My requests to the Guards for the legal representation to which I am entitled are routinely ignored. I don't actually have my own lawyer (though in my line of business I should), but as a citizen of Turai the state is meant to provide me with a Public Defender. They don't. It's well into the evening before anyone official pays me any attention at all. Two Guards thrust the door open and take me along a corridor into an interview room where Deputy Prefect Prasius is sitting stony faced behind a desk.

I'm moderately pleased to see Prasius. He doesn't like me any better than the Prefect, but he's not quite as stupid. He's younger than his boss Galwinius, and well spoken, as you would expect. You don't get promoted or elected into official posts in Turai unless you're well born and your name ends in the aristocratic '-ius'. A name like Thraxas marks you out as low born. There is no legal reason why a man from the lower classes can't be elected to high office, but the aristocrats have the Senate pretty much sewn up with money and patronage and it's extremely rare for a new man to break through.

'So, Thraxas. You want to tell us what you were doing in Thalius's house?'

'You want to tell me where my Public Defender is?'

Prasius looks round at his Guards. 'He wants to know where his Public Defender is. Anyone seen his Public Defender?'

The Guards shake their heads, which makes the fancy tassels on the shoulders of their tunics sway back and forward.

'Looks like no one's seen him.'

'I've a right to representation.'

'You've a right to shut up about lawyers and start answering questions. Now, what were you doing in Thalius's house? And why did you attack his daughter Soolanius?'

I lean forward and stare at him.

'Prasius. Is it a qualification for every official in this city that they have to be as dumb as an Orc? Do you really think you can intimidate me? Go to hell. Bring me my representative, and I might talk. Or I might not. Depends how I feel. Meanwhile, you better just take me back to the cell. If you want to keep holding me illegally, then do it. I'll expect a fat payment when I haul you through the law courts.'

This is not the way to talk to the Deputy Prefect if you want to get out of jail, but I'm damned if I'll ever knuckle under to these people. I'm taken back to my cell. My fellow prisoner is still lying on his bunk and he doesn't look any happier.

Later on I pay a Guard to give me today's copy of *The Renowned and Truthful Chronicle of All the World's Events*. There's nothing much in it unless you happen to be interested in the current leading scandal about the Senator's wife and the Army Captain, which I'm not. And the editor spends some time lambasting the Civil Guard for its inefficiency in not being able to find a two-ton statue. The statue of Saint Quatinius was meant to be dedicated at an important religious ceremony next month, attended by delegates from various other city-states. The paper fulminates over the fact that anyone could fail to find such an enormous object, and hints strongly that bribery and corruption must be involved. Fair enough, although I haven't had any more success than the Guards, and no one's bribing me.

Twelve Seas gets a mention on the back page, with a small news item on the burning down of one of our local taverns, the Boar's Head, and the death in the fire of the landlord, Trinex.

Lousy tavern, the Boar's Head, full of dwa dealers and exotic dancers. I won't miss it at all. I never liked Trinex either. The tavern was run by the Brotherhood and Trinex was a member of their organisation, which makes the affair interesting. The Brotherhood doesn't like it when one of their money-making establishments gets burned down. Very bad for business.

I'm used to being in a cell – it's happened to me enough times – so it doesn't particularly bother me, but it's frustrating to know that I've got nowhere with Grosex and time is running short. After doing the standard magical tests the Guard Sorcerer detected Grosex's aura on the knife. Only his aura, no one else's. And that's enough to convince the Guards and probably a jury that the apprentice killed the sculptor. The city law courts can push through a capital case in five days if they have the inclination. Unless I find out who really killed Drantaax then Grosex could be hanged in less than a week. And when I'm freed I'll be no further on really. I can't recognise the white villa the kuriya pool showed me. Even if I could there's no guarantee that Drantaax's wife would be there. I seem to be drawing a blank on this one.

I mull over what happened at the house of the Sorcerer Thalius. Even though I have no involvement in the case it's a curious chain of events. Why was it said that he was poisoned by a servant, when his daughter says he was murdered by a dwa dealer? And was he really killed by a crossbow bolt? That's a very unusual weapon in Turai. It's illegal to carry one inside the city walls. Although I recently encountered a very deadly crossbow killer named Sarin the Merciless who had some involvement in the dwa trade. I wonder if she might be back in Turai? I'd be interested to meet her again. She's a wanted woman and I'm always keen to collect a little reward money.

Most interesting of all, in view of my recent experiences, is the appearance of the monks. What were they doing there? Connected with the dwa trade? That wouldn't be a surprise. Practically everyone else in the city brushes up against dwa since it took over so many people's lives. But it could be something else entirely. Maybe Thalius had some religious artefact they wanted? But Thalius was strictly a small-time Sorcerer, unlikely to be in possession of anything very important. Maybe they just came to get their horoscopes read.

I wonder who the two groups were and why they were fighting. It's an odd coincidence that one day I find two strange monks burgling my rooms and the next thing you know there are monks slugging it out on the lawns in Thamlin. I speculate on what I might have blundered into, but I can't think of anything to fit the facts. I don't know much about warrior monks. There again, who does?

I spend the night in the cells. The next day it's hot as Orcish hell. The food is not what I'd call fit for humans and I'm desperate for a beer. I'm about to vent my frustration by kicking the door when it opens and Thalius's daughter walks in. She's steadier on her feet but I can tell she's been drinking. I'm not a man who'd condemn her for it. If you can't have a drink when your father gets murdered, when can you?

'Thraxas. They tell me you really are an Investigator. I thought you were another crook.'

She'd woken up from her prolonged drinking bout to find her house being searched by monks in red robes. Naturally this was disconcerting. She apologises for trying to stab me and I wave it away.

'Finding monks burgling your house is enough to unsettle anyone. Believe me, I know.'

She gets to the point quickly. The Guards are getting nowhere with the death of her father and she wants to hire me.

I glance round at my cellmate. He seems to be sleeping but I don't want to discuss anything in front of him. It's not beyond the intelligence of Deputy Prefect Prasius to have put one of his own men in here to spy on me.

'I'll take the job, but we can't discuss it here. You'll have to get me out of this cell first.'

She takes a small flask from her bag and sips from it. She's a pretty young woman, with a mass of dark hair and striking green eyes. Pretty enough to compliment were I not too old, overweight and generally washed up to be handing out compliments to young women.

'Can I get you out?'

'Sure. Just tell the Deputy Prefect I was in your house by your invitation. They don't have anything else to hold me on.'

This goes smoothly enough. Deputy Prefect Prasius makes me wait while he consults with Galwinius. They don't like it at all, but if Soolanis says she invited me in there's nothing they can do about it. I wasn't committing any other crime. Eventually a Guards Sorcerer accompanies us to the front entrance where he utters the necessary spell to open the door. I walk out into the scorching sunlight.

'I need a beer.'

So does Soolanis. We stop off in a tavern on the edge of Thamlin, a higher-class establishment than I would normally frequent. The landlord looks at me suspiciously but seems reassured by the presence of the obviously well-bred Soolanis until she starts knocking back glasses of klee in a manner quite unbecoming to a lady. Eventually I have to bundle her back into a landus and we head south.

Turning into Quintessence Street we pass the still smouldering ruins of the Boar's Head. Not a timber is left standing. Whoever set it alight did a good job, not that it's too hard to start a fire among rickety wooden buildings of Twelve Seas dried out by the fierce summer sun. Fire is a continual danger in the city. It's probably only because the space beside the tavern had already been cleared prior to reconstruction that there wasn't a far larger conflagration. Casax, the local Brotherhood boss, and Ixkar, a senior official in the Innkeepers Guild, are standing next to the ruins, grim-faced. They don't look like they're discussing plans for a summer outing. I wouldn't like to be the arsonist when they get hold of him.

Soolanis is half asleep as we ride to the Avenging Axe. She only makes it up the outside stairs with some difficulty. Once inside she slumps on to my couch and falls fast asleep. I stare at her with some frustration. She might at least have stayed awake long enough to pay me my retainer.

I have a large jug of water in my bedroom. I walk through to throw some on my face. The jug is empty and there's a young whore asleep in my bed. I know she's a whore because of the red ribbons in her hair. I've never seen her before.

I go looking for Makri. Makri comes looking for me and we meet at my door. She glances at Soolanis, sprawled out on my couch.

'You finally found a girlfriend who drinks as much as you.'

'Very amusing. Who the hell is that in my bed?'

'In your bed? Right. That'll be Quen, I expect. She's a whore.'

'I know she's a whore. I saw the ribbons. Is this some kind of joke?'

Makri shifts a little uncomfortably. 'I wasn't expecting you back just yet. I thought you might be longer in prison . . .'

I explode. 'Damn help you are, Makri. Other people might do something like finding me a lawyer to get me out of jail. Not you. You fill my room with whores and hope I won't be back for a while. Get her out of there!'

'I can't,' wails Makri, and starts to look distressed. 'Everyone's after her.'

'Who's everyone?'

'The Guards. And the Brotherhood. And the Innkeepers Guild.'

A horrible suspicion starts to form in my mind. 'You don't mean she . . .'

Makri nods. 'She burned down the Boar's Head. But she didn't mean to kill the landlord. She was just teaching him a lesson.'

'Well she certainly taught him a good one. Okay,

now I know who she is. I still don't know what she's doing here.'

'She just turned up. In a panic. She was looking for me. We met before, at a meeting.'

I gaze at Makri with horror. 'You knew her before? And she came into the downstairs bar? She just walked in after burning down the Boar's Head only a hundred yards away? And you led her up here? Why didn't you just put up a big sign saying *Wanted: arsonist hiding in Thraxas's room*? Get her out of here this second!'

'But she's safe here.'

'She is far from safe. The Brotherhood has eyes everywhere. God knows how many people will have seen her come in here. And even if no one did, the Brotherhood will use a Sorcerer. Ten to one Casax has one of them working on it now.'

Makri was unaware that the Boar's Head was owned by the Brotherhood. She realises that it makes it more serious. Not that it would be any light matter if it was just Civil Guards and the Innkeepers Guild in pursuit. Like most guilds, the innkeepers have some powerful connections.

'What can we do to help her?'

'You can do what you like, Makri. I'm doing nothing. Just get her out of here. And quickly.'

'But the landlord assaulted her!'

'I sympathise. It must be a hard life as an exotic dancer. Now, are you going to get rid of her or do I have to throw her out myself?'

Gurd rattles the door and sticks his head in.

'Thraxas. The Guards are downstairs looking for you. You want me to stall them?'

I nod. He departs.

There's a fierce banging at my outside door.

'Thraxas,' comes a voice I wish I didn't recognise. 'It's Casax. I need to talk to you.'

Well, that's fine. The Guards are downstairs and the local Brotherhood boss is outside. I glare at Makri with loathing. She shrugs, and draws a long knife from her boot.

'Got an axe anywhere?'

One thing you can't take away from Makri, she's always prepared to make her death stand. Personally, I need a little more notice.

'Stall him,' I say, and start rummaging in my bag for the spell of bafflement I borrowed from Astrath Triple Moon.

Casting a spell for the first time is no simple matter. It takes time, thought and preparation. However, with Gurd holding off the Guards downstairs and Makri stalling Casax by pretending she doesn't speak the language very well, there's no time for any of that. I just drag out the scroll, hurry into my bedroom and chant it out over the sleeping form of Quen. Nothing happens, not even the customary cooling of the surrounding air when magic is used, so whether it's worked or not is anybody's guess. By the time I get back to my office Prefect Tholius is clumping through the inside door with six Guards in his trail and a very angry Casax is confronting Makri at the steps with some of his brutes.

Casax, the boss of the Brotherhood in Twelve Seas, is new to the job. He was Yubaxas's number two and took over the leadership when Yubaxas was killed a couple of months ago by the Society of Friends, the Brotherhood's rivals, who run the north of the city. Casax is keen to assert his authority and he is not pleased to have been kept waiting.

'Who is this squeeze that doesn't speak the language?' he demands, which makes Makri frown. Being called a squeeze is not something she enjoys.

'It's his Orcish friend,' says Karlox. Karlox is a Brotherhood enforcer, a massive man, stupid, aggressive and hostile. Casax, no angel himself, stares round the room suspiciously.

Prefect Tholius meanwhile is unsure of how to proceed. As Prefect of the Twelve Seas, he should in theory be in charge here but he knows that in practice he can't order Casax around. Wishing neither to offend the Brotherhood boss nor to acknowledge his inferiority to Casax, the Prefect looks perplexed.

Casax is far from confused. He's a dangerous character and looks it: large, muscular, never known to smile. He's around forty, with long black hair tied back neatly in a braid, a plain brown tunic and a large gold hoop dangling from each ear. Unlike some gang bosses he doesn't go in for ostentation and apart from the earrings he wears no jewellery. His sword is sheathed in a plain black scabbard. He rose through the ranks of the Brotherhood, which doesn't happen unless you're smart and ruthless.

'We're looking for a woman named Quen.'

'Never heard of her. You know anyone called Quen, Makri?'

Makri shakes her head. She has her knife in her hand and she's madder than a mad Sorcerer about Karlox calling her an Orc. It wouldn't take too much now for her to attack them all and damn the consequences. If they find Quen and try to take her away, she certainly will.

Casax signals and his followers start searching. The Brotherhood boss greets Prefect Tholius without showing much respect, and enquires what brings him here.

'We are also seeking the woman called Quen. On a charge of murder and arson.'

Casax grunts. 'After we've got hold of her there won't be much left for a trial.'

'Who is this?' demands Tholius, motioning to Soolanis, still slumbering peacefully on the couch.

'A client.'

'Your clients always sleep in here?'

'Only when they get tired.'

The Brotherhood men enter my bedroom, followed by two Civil Guards. My heart is pounding. I mentally snarl a curse at Makri. If she had to bring a murderer and arsonist here, why did it have to be one who'd offended so many important people? Between the Brotherhood and the Civil Guards, I'm finished in this city. Things couldn't be worse if I'd challenged the King to single combat. Rivers of sweat drench my body.

I conceal my nerves. I've no more desire than Makri

to bow down to these people. The Brotherhood might be stronger than me but I'm never going to treat its thugs with respect. I grab a bottle of klee from my cupboard and take a hefty slug, then offer it to Makri as if there was nothing wrong at all.

Casax is staring at me. 'You drink too much, fat man.'

'Is that so?'

The searchers emerge from the bedroom. One of the Brotherhood men starts to speak but seems to forget how to. The other does it for him.

'In sir no one.'

'What the hell d'you mean, "In sir no one"?' rasps Casax, scowling.

The man shakes his head. 'I mean no one in there, sir.'

One of the Civil Guards nods in agreement.

'Search the rest of the tavern,' orders Casax. Prefect Tholius instructs his men to do the same.

What do you know? The spell of bafflement worked. No stranger entering the room can find Quen.

Casax strides over to confront me. He towers over me. His skin is bad. 'If you're hiding the whore, you're in big trouble, Thraxas. She burned down one of our places. Killed one of my men. The Brotherhood can't allow that sort of thing to happen.'

'But you can allow one of your men to seriously assault a young woman,' says Makri, striding over in turn to confront Casax. He shrugs.

'Part of the job.'

'Really? I work in a bar too. Try sending some of

your men over here to assault me.' Makri's eyes narrow slightly. She's still gripping her knife. Casax is surprised to find himself confronted by a young woman, but unperturbed.

'I've heard of you. You must be Makri. Part Human. Part Elf. Part Orc. You got pointed ears under all that hair?'

'Why don't you take a look?' says Makri, who would certainly gut him if he tried.

Casax grins. 'I hear you're a good fighter. Very good with a blade. But don't get ideas above your station. You're wasting your talents here, you know. Come and work for me. Earn you a lot more money. Maybe pay for the University.'

Karlox guffaws at the idea of Makri going to University, but I'm not entirely sure that Casax's offer isn't serious.

Makri looks slightly disconcerted to learn that Casax knows so much about her. She doesn't reply. She keeps her knife in her hand and her attention on her enemies.

'Sorcerer traced the whore to this tavern, Thraxas.'

'Maybe he was mistaken. The Brotherhood don't use magic often, do they?'

'We use it when we have to. Now, where is she?'

'I've never seen her.'

Annoyance flickers over the Boss's face. After the search of the tavern produces no results there is a moment of tension while he stares at us as if making up his mind whether to order his thugs to attack us there and then. He decides against it.

Before leaving Casax informs us that we will be under surveillance and if we are found to be sheltering Quen then he'll kill us. He says this quite matter-of-factly.

'No doubt Prefect Tholius will protect me with the full weight of the law,' I suggest.

The Prefect leaves without saying anything.

When they've all left Makri thanks me for helping and apologises for landing me in this mess. I wave it away. I'm too worn out to be angry any more.

'Anyway, it's good to put one over on the Brotherhood. It bugs me the way they're always going round like they're number one chariot around here.'

'I thought they were.'

'Well it annoys me anyway.'

Soolanis has slept though all of this and shows no sign of coming to life. I explain who she is to Makri, and wonder out loud what we're going to do with Quen. We certainly can't move her right now, yet it is very unsafe for her to stay. My bafflement spell isn't going to fool a prying Sorcerer for long, though it's true that the Brotherhood generally rely on muscle and fear rather than magic and may not be using a top-class Wizard.

'Incidentally, Makri, why did you put her in my bed? Wouldn't she be more comfortable in your room?'

Before Makri can answer the door opens. Dandelion appears.

'Did you persuade him yet?' she says.

'There wasn't room,' explains Makri. 'I, eh . . . said Dandelion could stay for a while.'

I groan. Dandelion starts talking about dolphins but I'm already on my way downstairs.

'A beer, Gurd, and quickly.'

'Trouble with the Brotherhood?' says Gurd, seeing the shaky state I'm in.

'I can cope with the Brotherhood,' I tell him. 'It's the sisterhood that's getting to me.'

CHAPTER
SIX

I need to send a message to Astrath Triple Moon to see if we can do anything to boost the spell of bafflement to keep Quen hidden till we decide what to do about her. I can't go myself. Walking straight out of here and round to a friendly Sorcerer would be a sure sign of what I was up to. The same goes for Makri, and anyway she doesn't want to miss her afternoon lecture in rhetoric. Gurd and Tanrose can't leave the bar and Palax and Kaby are out busking on the streets. Which is the sum total of people I can trust.

'Dandelion could go,' suggests Makri.

I let forth some abuse about Dandelion, pointing out that a woman who walks around Turai in bare feet with flowers in her hair is likely to be as much use as a one-legged gladiator when it comes to practical matters.

'She casts horoscopes for dolphins, for God's sake.'

'The Brotherhood won't suspect her.'

True enough. We send Dandelion with the message.

'You know, Makri, two days ago I was sitting here without a care in the world. How did all this happen?'

'You got annoyed because Prefect Tholius dragged Grosex out of your room.'

So I did. Foolish of me. I didn't need to do anything. Wasn't even hired to do anything. And now I'm looking for a two-ton statue and trying to find the wife of a murdered sculptor. Which led me into the affair of Thalius Green Eye and his inebriated daughter, again entirely my own fault.

'But Quen was nothing to do with me. You landed me in that one. What did the landlord do to her anyway?'

Makri doesn't want to go into details, though she seems satisfied that burning down his tavern and him in the process was a reasonable act of retaliation. She's hopeful that if she can protect her from her immediate danger then some of the more powerful women in the Association of Gentlewomen will look after her, maybe providing funds for her to leave Turai and set up somewhere else.

Soolanis finally wakes just as Makri is taking her leave, wrapped in the large cloak she is obliged to wear at the Guild College. Her chainmail bikini proved to be far too distracting for young students and old professors alike, and even her man's tunic showed off too much of her legs, apparently.

'What's the matter with these people?' complains Makri. 'If it's not one thing it's another. Now I have to sit at the back of the class wrapped up like a mummy just because they can't concentrate on the lesson.'

Soolanis needs a drink. I pass her some water. If she wants to drink herself to death that's her affair, but I need her to stay sober long enough to tell me some details of the case. She drinks the water with the same lack of enthusiasm I might show in the same circumstances.

'Where did you get that?' she asks abruptly, rising to her feet and pointing at Makri's purse.

'I took it from the neck of a man I killed.'

'It's my father's,' says Soolanis. 'It has his name embroidered on it.'

I study the purse. And indeed, the name of Thalius Green Eye is embroidered in tiny letters in one of the arcane magic languages normally reserved for spells. It's something I should have spotted earlier, though the writing is very small and intertwined with the rest of the needlework.

Soolanis is highly agitated. Myself, I'm puzzled. What's the connection between the man who walked into the bar and tried to kill me, and Thalius Green Eye?

I ask Makri to leave the purse behind, and she does so. Quen is still sleeping in my bedroom. I leave her be for the moment, but when night comes she's going to have to go and struggle for space in Makri's room. I surrender my bed for no one. And I don't share it with anyone, either.

'All right, Soolanis. Tell me everything you know about your father's death.'

Soolanis tells me that Thalius was always in trouble with money. He was a minor figure at the Imperial Palace, outshone by the talents of the other Sorcerers, and even his business of drawing up horoscopes for lesser aristocrats was on the wane. It's expensive living in Thamlin and the upkeep of his villa in Truth is Beauty Lane soon led him into debt.

'He didn't know where to turn. So he turned to dwa.'

The dwa made him forget his problems but the natural consequence was that his problems worsened. Less work, more expense. He couldn't even face going to the Palace unless he was full of dwa, and when he made it there he was in no state to draw up a horoscope.

'After a while it took over his life.'

I get the impression that somewhere at that time drink took over for Soolanis. When the neighbours started talking about Thalius she found it almost impossible to face the world without fortifying herself.

Despite the poor state Thalius was reduced to, he was never forbidden to enter the Palace, which suggests that he might have been taking something there that someone important wanted quite badly. Prince Frisen-Akan has already been in trouble because of his liking for dwa.

'You think your father was killed because he couldn't pay his dealer?'

'Probably. That's what happens, isn't it?'

She claims not to know who his dealer was. Because Thalius was killed by a crossbow I question her about Sarin the Merciless, but the name doesn't ring a bell and she doesn't recognise my description of her. For the past four months she's been so obliterated by alcohol that she can't recollect much of what's been going on around her.

She looks sadly at the small purse. 'He liked this. Never let it out of his sight. Do you have any wine?'

I shake my head. I never developed a taste for it. I take her a beer, which serves just as well.

'I'd say it was unusual for a Sorcerer to be killed over a dwa debt. Not impossible, but the dealer would rather have the money, and there must have been stuff in the house your father could have sold. Unless it wasn't just a small debt for his own dwa. Perhaps he owed much more. Was he dealing himself?'

The thought of her father actually dealing dwa brings tears to Soolanis's eyes. She admits that it's possible, but she doesn't know.

I muse on these things. If Thalius was a rather larger player in dwa than his daughter realised it might explain why the Guards have covered up the facts of the case. Drug scandals have already come too close to the Palace, particularly in the person of Prince Frisen-Akan, and the authorities wouldn't want any more trouble. Consul Kalius has already had to hide the Prince's shortcomings from the public. The politics of Turai are in a perpetually fragile state and Senator Lodius, the leader of the anti-royalist Populares, is always quick to pounce on any scandal he can use for his own ends.

Prince Frisen-Akan is keen on dwa and I have no doubt that he's not the only one among his circle who is. If Thalius Green Eye was supplying them it would explain why he wasn't thrown out of the Palace and also how he might have accrued enough debts to get himself killed. Taking a shipment of dwa and failing to make the payment is a stupid thing to do, but it happens surprisingly often, with inevitable results.

I'm considering the possibilities of Thalius taking dwa into the Palace when an odd thought occurs. Why was he so fond of the purse? This one is nothing special. All sort of things can have sentimental value, but I don't recall meeting anyone who was overly attached to their purse.

I study it. It's small and the top fastens with two drawstrings, the sort of thing for holding a few gurans. No room for anything else. I mutter a word in the old Sorcerers' language, a common word for commanding something to open. I sense a fractional cooling in the air. I draw on the two strings and the purse opens, and keeps opening. It opens an impossible amount.

Soolanis gapes in astonishment as I draw the small mouth of the purse further and further apart till it eventually reaches the length of my outstretched arms.

'What is it?' she asks, disconcerted by the impossibility of what she's seeing.

'The magic space,' I reply. 'Or rather an opening into the magic space. Another dimension, whatever that means. This is no ordinary purse. It's a magic pocket.'

I look into the large hole I have now opened. My face goes cold as it nears the interface between the normal world and the magic space. Inside everything is tinged with a purple hue and my eyes take a while to adjust.

Anything put in magic space to all intents and purposes will lose all weight and volume. Which would be a very handy way for a Sorcerer to take a large bag of dwa into the Palace for instance. My eyes adjust to the odd light. I reach down, stretching my whole arm into the purse. Anyone looking on would think that my limb was vanishing into thin air. I'm expecting my fingers to settle in soft-powdered dwa. Instead they encounter something hard, cold and metallic. I take my hand out and look again. It's a head. A bronze head. With a body attached. And it's sitting on a horse.

I withdraw my head from the magic space and look at the purse in my hand. Even for a man who's used to magic, it is very strange to realise that I am at this moment holding a two-ton statue of Saint Quatinius right in the palm of my hand.

'Well, that explains a lot,' I mutter.

I'm fairly pleased with myself. The Guards are looking all over the city for this. Sorcerers at the Abode of Justice have been hunting for it. And I've found it. Which, I believe, means a handsome reward is now owing to me. Well done, Thraxas. Not only have you found the statue, you've enabled the religious ceremony to go ahead and also smoothed over a very awkward breakdown in relations between Turai and Nioj. They might even give you a medal.

More importantly, I've probably found Drantaax's killers. If the two men who arrived in the Avenging Axe were carrying his statue it seems a safe bet they killed him to get it. Too late to question them but with the Sorcerers at the Abode of Justice that's not always necessary. If they were at Drantaax's workshop there's a strong chance a few things like dust will have stuck to them. A good Sorcerer will be able to pin it down, linking them to the crime. I just have to get the bodies examined.

I waste no time. The bodies, once deposited in Quintessence Street, were picked up by the public refuse service. I informed the Guards of what had happened but, for a pair of known crooks, the Guards won't have taken much trouble. The bodies will have been sent to the morgue in Twelve Seas for burial or cremation. Fortunately for me, there's been a backlog ever since the riots. Beggars who die in the streets now have to wait up to two weeks before it's their turn to go.

Captain Rallee is at his Guard station. When I tell him I think I've found Drantaax's killers he's full of questions, most of which I decline to answer.

'So it just so happens that the two guys who attacked you in the Avenging Axe also killed Drantaax?' he grunts, suspiciously. 'How come you just discovered that?'

'Can't reveal my sources, Captain. You know that. It won't matter to you anyway when we get the bodies checked and they turn out to be the killers. It'll be a feather in your cap. Also, it'll put Grosex in the clear.'

The Captain says he'll believe it when he sees it. We take the short walk to the morgue. The Captain sends the attendant through to the back to check his files.

'I still reckon the apprentice did it.'

'That poor little guy? Come on, Captain, does he look like a murderer to you?'

'Yes.'

After some time, the morgue attendant comes back. 'Cremated the bodies yesterday.'

My jaw drops in a foolish manner. 'Yesterday? What do you mean yesterday? There's a two-week delay.'

'Not any more. Prefect Tholius provided us with the funds for more workers. We've been clearing up the backlog. The Consul figured it was time we got this city back in order after the riots.'

I turn to the Captain. 'But they did it.'

The Captain raises an eyebrow. 'And now they're gone. Very convenient, Thraxas. Look, I know you have to try and clear your client, but I'm a busy man. I don't have time for this. If you have a fight with some other thug and he miraculously turns out to be Drantaax's killer as well, don't tell me about it.'

The Captain thinks I've made the whole thing up. Probably suspects I checked that they were cremated first before coming to him with my theory.

'You were a good soldier, Thraxas, but as an Investigator you're about as much use as a eunuch in a brothel.'

He departs, leaving me frustrated, cursing my luck that the Consul should at this moment decide to assign more money to the city's morgues. If these two did kill Drantaax all traces of the connection have now gone up in smoke. I trudge back to the Avenging Axe. What to do?

I still have the statue but that isn't much use any more. There seemed an excellent chance it would carry decisive clues to the murderer of Drantaax. During their manhandling, the killer or his accomplices would have left traces of their auras which a Sorcerer could detect. Not now though. The aura will have been irretrievably washed away in the magic space. From what I remember of my lore physical objects survive unscathed in the magic space, but all magic vanishes, including remnants of auras. Spectacular find or not, it hasn't moved me any closer to clearing Grosex. With my number one suspects now gone, I'm not sure how I'm ever going to clear him.

'Just keep digging around, I guess,' I mutter to no one in particular as I order a beer. Thinking about it, even if the two newly departed crooks were in on it, I doubt if they masterminded the whole operation.

Soolanis is at the bar, so I ask her a few more questions.

'Where did your father get that purse?'

Soolanis doesn't know. She thinks he brought it back with him from his travels in the west when he was a young man.

'It's an extremely rare item. You know it's illegal to have one in Turai? As far as I know there are only two in the city and they're both owned by the King. If Thalius had been caught with this he'd have ended up rowing a prison trireme.'

They're banned because they make the King nervous. Too easy to seek an audience then suddenly pull a sword out of thin air. It wouldn't be the first time a King had been assassinated that way. I suppose Thalius was safe enough using it to take dwa into the palace. Magic purses like this can be detected by Sorcerers, but only with difficulty, and only if they're looking for it. Who would expect a wash-out like Thalius to have such a rare and valuable item?

Soolanis finishes her beer and looks around for another.

'So, Soolanis, it looks like whoever killed your father also killed Drantaax. I had a couple of suspects but I can't get to them now. Maybe someone else was in on it. Did anyone know he had this purse?'

Soolanis doesn't know. She doesn't know much about anything. All she wants to do is drink. The Avenging Axe is home from home for her. I offer to call a landus to take her back to Thamlin. She says she'd like to stay a while. As a Sorcerer's daughter from Thamlin, she's never been to a tavern on the wrong side of town before. She likes it.

'I've never had beer before. We always had wine at home.'

I leave her to her beer and climb the stairs to my office. As I enter a knock comes at my outside door. I ask who it is. It turns out to be three monks. Unlike the last ones that visited, they ask politely if they can enter. They're wearing yellow robes. I figure that's okay. It was the red ones that burgled me. I let them in. Two young monks, plus one old and venerable. The young ones stand respectfully as I clear some junk off a chair for their master to sit down. Despite his obvious great age he walks quickly and easily, and when he sits his back is straight as a broomstick.

He greets me in a voice far stronger than you'd expect from such an old man. This is a man who's lived a healthy life. I doubt if he's ever drunk beer or smoked thazis.

'Forgive us for calling without sending warning of our coming. We are not often in the city and felt it was best to take the chance of finding you home.'

Politeness always makes me suspicious. I stare at him. 'How can I help you?'

'We wish to hire you to find a statue,' says the venerable monk.

Now there's a coincidence. And me with a large statue right here in my pocket. 'Tell me about it,' I say.

CHAPTER
SEVEN

The old monk is called Tresius. The Venerable Tresius. The others are not introduced. I'm not sure if the two younger monks were among the ones I saw fighting outside Thalius's house. With their shaved heads and yellow robes they all look much the same. I don't mention the incident. Neither do they.

Tresius tells an interesting tale in a sonorous voice reminding me of a kindly old Sorcerer I used to take instruction from. He taught me how to levitate. Between the ages of fifteen and sixteen I could raise myself four inches off the ground. Didn't last for long. I seem to remember I lost the art almost immediately after having my first beer.

'We are members of the Cloud Temple. We live and practise in a monastery in the hills.'

I nod. Various isolated religious establishments are found in the far northern hills that border on Nioj, though it's a long time since I was up there, fifteen years or so, during the last war with Nioj, in fact. The thought evokes some powerful memories. Turai was stronger then, and not just because I was in the Army. All citizens were obliged to do military service. We used to be proud to do it. A man couldn't get anywhere in this city unless he'd fought for his country. Now half the population bribes their way out and King Reeth-Akan hires mercenaries instead. Many of our Senators have never even held a sword. A generation ago that was unheard of. It'll lead us into trouble one day.

I remember the day far up in the hills when we fought the invading Niojan troops to a standstill, destroying one legion and then another. We were holding out at a pass. Captain Rallee was there, a young soldier like me. We stood in our phalanx with our long spears in our hands and when they were broken we kept them at bay with our swords. We would have driven them back completely if more of their legions hadn't made it through another pass and outflanked us. After that it was a bloody retreat and a desperate fight right outside the walls of our city. And even there we held them off despite the huge superiority of their forces. The Niojan Army was four times the size of ours, even then.

Finally we were driven back into the city and were under siege with ladders and towers at every wall, fighting for our lives. Our Sorcerers exhausted their spells and took up weapons to join the defenders. So did the city's women. Even children joined in, hurling stones and slates from the walls at the sea of enemies swarming up from below. And then, just as the Niojans were starting to spill over our walls, news came that the Orcs had invaded from the east, rolling over the Wastelands with the largest army ever seen in the history of the world. Orcs, Half-Orcs, Trolls, Dragons,

Sorcerers, unnamed beasts, everything they could gather under the leadership of Bhergaz the Fierce, the last great Orcish warrior chief to unite all their nations, all heading west with the intention of wiping us off the face of the earth. So the war between Turai, the League of City-States and Nioj ended abruptly as everyone combined in another desperate campaign to drive the vast Orcish Army back. Captain Rallee and I found ourselves fighting shoulder to shoulder with Niojans that only yesterday had been trying to kill us.

The Orc Wars were long and bloody. Battles raged on our borders and around our cities for months. With the help of the Elves we finally drove them out but at great cost. The population of some states has never recovered and several once fine cities are deserted ruins. There's been an uneasy peace ever since. We've even signed a treaty with the Orcs, and exchanged Ambassadors, but it won't last. It never does. Orcs and Humans hate each other too much. The Orcs waste their energy fighting among themselves, but once another leader powerful enough to unite them comes along, they'll be back.

It's barren land, around the hills. Cooler than the city though. Probably quite a suitable spot for meditating. I banish the wartime memories from my mind and concentrate on the monk's tale.

Most of the religious establishments up there are branches of the True Church, the state religion of Turai, but a few fall outside its authority. As Turai is more liberal in religious matters than some other states this is generally not a problem, providing they don't go around spouting heresies and spreading unrest. If that happens the King sends up a battalion and expels them from the country. I guess we're not that liberal in religious matters. I haven't heard of the Cloud Temple before.

'We have only been established for a short time. Until last year myself and the other monks were brothers of the Star Temple. Unfortunately there was a falling-out. I will not go into details – the disagreements were of a theological nature. While of great importance to us, they are not really relevant.'

'Let me decide what's relevant.'

'Very well. The dispute hinged around a debate on the nature of consubstantiality, concerning the exact way in which the Divinity relates to the substance of which the temporal world is made.'

'Okay, skip the details. What happened after you started arguing?'

'Great bitterness arose, leading to divisions among us. There was even a danger of fighting. We are, as you may know, warriors as well as monks. The ability to fight is part of our spiritual training, disciplining us for the rigours of worship and sacrifice. Eventually, to bring an end to the terrible dispute, myself and some others left the Star Temple to found our own monastery, well away from our former brothers.'

Tresius had been number two monk in the Star Temple, whose Abbot was Ixial the Seer. The way Tresius tells it, this parting of the ways went smoothly enough, but I have my doubts. Even if he's next best thing to a saint, no Abbot is going to like it if half of his monks suddenly go off and worship somewhere else.

I have my suspicions about the real cause of the schism. In my experience of human nature – admittedly based on a knowledge of the lowest forms – fancy disputes about fine points of detail in any organisation are liable just to be excuses for a good fight about who's really in charge. The way I read the situation, Tresius challenged Ixial the Seer for leadership and the result was too close to call, so he quit, along with half the monks.

I'm getting bored with this tale of quarrelling monastics when Tresius finally reaches the interesting part.

'During the struggle that took place before we left, the statue of Saint Quatinius that stood in the courtyard of the monastery was toppled from its pedestal and destroyed. This was a bitter blow for everyone. The statue was an ancient and beautiful work, carved in marble from the quarries of Juval. It is vital for a monastery of warrior monks to have in its possession a statue of Saint Quatinius.'

Quatinius was a fighting saint, killed at war with the Orcs some hundreds of years ago. Warrior monks consequently regard him as an inspiration for their calling.

'We of the Cloud Temple did of course face the founding of our new monastery without such a statue. But we were aware of that, and have already commissioned the sculpting of a new one. Marble is no longer imported from Juval, so we commissioned one of bronze from Drantaax.'

I raise my eyebrows.

'It would have taken some months to complete, but now that Drantaax is dead we will be forced to recommission it elsewhere, which will of course mean a delay. Sculptors of his skill are rare, and always have work already in hand. For our fledgling monastery, this delay is a serious setback. Are you aware of the Triple-Moon Conjunction in three months' time?'

I am. I still remember enough of my sorcerous training to recall the most important astrological phenomena. When the three moons line up in the sky every ten years or so, it's a major event. We have a festival. Everyone sings hymns and gets drunk at the chariot races. I've always enjoyed it.

'If we do not have a statue at the time of the conjunction it will mean a serious loss of face.'

'How serious?'

The Venerable Tresius turns his head to his two followers and makes some slight movement with his eyes. They bow, and depart. Left alone, he inclines his head towards me.

'Very serious indeed. We cannot perform our Conjunction ritual without it. If Ixial the Seer has replaced his own statue by then, monks from the Cloud Temple may be placed in a difficult situation.'

'In plain language, no statue, no monks?'

He nods.

'But Ixial and the Star Temple don't have a statue either. Have they commissioned a new one?'

'I believe not. I believe that they are responsible for the theft from Drantaax.'

'Are you saying that Ixial, who's an Abbot, actually connived in the murder of Drantaax just so he could nab a statue for himself?'

'Quite possibly. Ixial is ruthless. I do not believe that his monks would have set out to commit murder but who knows what may have gone wrong when they tried to purloin the statue that was intended for the shrine? Alternatively, he may have hired others to do it for him, and been unaware of what might happen. Either way, with the twin events of the theft and the murder Ixial has struck a devastating blow against me. Drantaax's death means that our own icon will not be ready and he may gain an impressive new one for his own monastery. If that is the situation when the Triple-Moon Conjunction comes then his temple will gain dominance over ours.'

'Meaning you lose out?'

'Exactly. And I do not wish my followers to return to Ixial.'

I mull this over. I grab a beer from the crate on my shelf, open it, drink and mull it over some more.

'What exactly are you wanting to hire me to do? If I find the statue, I can't hand it over to you. It's being made for the shrine and it belongs to the city authorities.'

The Venerable Tresius is aware of this. He doesn't mind it being returned to the city authorities; he just doesn't want it going to Ixial. Apparently if no one has a statue that is not too bad. Of course if it turns out that Ixial was behind the murder and I prove it, then that removes Ixial and Tresius won't mind that at all.

'If he was not behind it, and you return the statue

to the city, then each of our temples may flourish according to our merits.'

'But if no one recovers the statue and it ends up at the Star Temple then your young monks will take a hike?'

He nods.

'You know I'm involved in this case already? I haven't been hired to find the statue, but I'm looking for the killer of Drantaax.'

'Is it not likely that in the course of your investigation into the murder you will find the statue?'

'Sure it's likely. I'll put Ixial in jail as well if it turns out he was responsible for killing the sculptor.'

The Venerable Tresius doesn't look too despondent at the thought of Ixial in jail. He gives the impression that Ixial is capable of anything. This consubstantiality argument must have been pretty bitter.

I ask him if he has any idea where the statue might be now. It's in my pocket of course, but I'm curious about how much Tresius knows.

'No, but I believe it has not yet reached the Star Temple.'

'Why?'

'I have means of obtaining information from that establishment.'

'You mean you have a spy there?'

He declines to answer this.

'So, basically, Tresius, you want to prevent Ixial from getting this statue. You're hiring me to find it and hand it back to the authorities.'

He nods. I don't see any reason not to take his

money. I'm going to hand it back to the authorities anyway, when I've finished with it.

I take my standard thirty-guran retainer.

I ask him if he's come across any of the Star Temple monks since he's been in Turai. He says that he hasn't. Which is a lie, given that I saw them fighting.

'One last thing. Why is he called Ixial the Seer? Is he a prophet?'

'Not exactly. But he does see very far in all directions. There is very little that he does not know.'

Tresius takes his leave. At the doorway he meets Dandelion.

'Nice robe,' says Dandelion, looking admiringly at the yellow cloth.

Tresius smiles serenely and departs, his warrior monk training providing him with enough inner strength not to flinch at Dandelion. Myself, I stare at her bare feet and flowers with renewed disgust.

'Astrath Triple Moon said to tell you that he is sure he can help,' she reports.

She liked Astrath. Particularly his rainbow cloak and the colourful hat he wears on special occasions.

'I'm not sure if he knows too much about the stars, though. He didn't believe me when I told him that everyone born under the sign of the dragon was going to have a lucky year. I promised I'd go back and talk to him about it.'

Poor Astrath.

Dandelion starts rambling on about the dolphins. Apparently they are really suffering without their healing stone. She can't understand why I won't help.

'They are very upset that you won't help them.'

'Oh yes? And how do you know that?'

'They told me, of course.'

The dolphins can't really talk. It's just a story for children. I get a bleak mental image of Dandelion at the seashore, gibbering in the direction of some bemused-looking dolphins. Poor dolphins. I tell her I'm busy and banish her from my office. I've got things to think about.

Grabbing this rare moment of peace and quiet, I consult my book of spells and load the sleep spell into my mind. It is an unfortunate facet of magic that the spells don't stay in your memory, no matter how good you are. Once you use them, they're gone, and you have to learn them all over again.

Once I have the sleep spell learned I feel better. I have an uncomfortable feeling that before too long I am going to be involved with a lot of warrior monks and after seeing them flying through the air aiming kicks at each other's heads, I've no intention of getting involved in hand-to-hand combat. Anyone aiming a flying kick at me is going to find himself sleeping soundly before he lands.

Quen appears. I intimate that she's about as welcome in my room as an Orc at an Elvish wedding, and throw her out.

'Go and hide in Makri's room. If you're short of space in there then sit on Dandelion's shoulders. See if she can predict how you're going to escape the city.'

I settle down with another beer, and think about things.

CHAPTER
EIGHT

When I tell Makri about Tresius she's impressed.
'It's your ideal case, Thraxas. Someone hires
you to find something you already have. I take it you'll
be spinning it out for a few weeks so you can charge
him more?'

'Very amusing, Makri. Guild College has improved
your sarcasm tremendously. The reason I didn't tell
him I had the statue is that I haven't finished with it
yet. I'm still trying to clear Grosex, remember. This is
evidence.'

Makri is even more impressed when I show her the
huge statue inside the small purse.

'I like the look of the magic space. Everything's
purple. Can we go in?'

'Definitely not. Entering the magic space is a very
bad thing to do. My old teacher forbade it.'

'You think this Ixial the Seer did kill Drantaax?' I've
been filling in Makri on the details.

'It looks like he might be behind it. Which is fine
with me. If I can prove it I'll get Grosex out of jail and
it'll be one in the eye for Prefect Tholius. But it doesn't
explain why the statue is here, though. Why did it end
up in that man's purse? If the thugs that tried to kill

me were working for Ixial, why didn't they give him the statue?'

'Maybe they just couldn't wait to attack you.'

'Possibly, I'm that kind of guy. But how come they had the purse with the statue?'

'Maybe just coincidence,' suggests Makri. 'They might have stolen it, or bought it in a tavern. After all, whoever took it from Thalius Green Eye might not have known what it was.'

This is possible. Bit of a coincidence, but it's not that unlikely that my old adversary robbed Thalius and then headed for Twelve Seas to lay low for a while. I'm not convinced though. I figure that Soolanis is wide of the mark when she says that her father was killed over a dwa debt. I reckon the purse was the main reason. Which makes his killer a very ruthless person, if he was murdered merely to provide a means of exporting a statue from the city without anyone noticing.

'I'm dealing with a brutal killer here, Makri. Murdered a Sorcerer and the city's top sculptor. You know Thalius was killed with a crossbow?'

'I thought he was poisoned by a servant.'

'Just a cover-up by the authorities. He was involved in dwa, probably taking it up to Prince Frisen-Akan at the palace. Consul Kalius won't want to reopen that scandal. It's only two months since the Prince's drug habit was nearly exposed to the population. Remember a ruthless killer with a fondness for crossbows?'

'Sure. Sarin the Merciless.'

Sarin the Merciless. I ran her out of town years ago when she was all mouth and no action. She showed up recently in a far more deadly fashion, having honed her fighting skills for four years in a monastery with a group of warrior monks. I remind Makri of the warrior monk connection and she agrees that we could be dealing with Sarin once again.

'You keen to meet her again after last time?'

'What do you mean "after last time"?' I demand.

'Didn't she win?'

I scoff at the suggestion. 'Win? Against me? Please. I only let her go because I was busy with other things, like saving the city from destruction. If she shows her face around here again I'll be down on her like a bad spell. Anyway, freeing her was a smart move. Boost the reward money when I nail her this time. No cropped-haired, crossbow-wielding killer is going to get away from me twice.'

Makri lights a thazis stick, inhales a few times and passes it to me. I pour us a little klee. Makri's eyes water as it burns her throat on the way down.

'Why do you drink this stuff?' she demands. 'We'd have rioted in the slave pits if they tried serving it to us.'

'This is top-quality klee. Another glass?'

'Okay.'

There's a commotion outside as a stonemason gets into an argument with an architect. I hear that the master craftsmen have been complaining to their guilds that they're being provided with sub-standard materials, which wouldn't be a surprise. The King opened up the public purse to pay for many of the repairs to the city but by the time the Praetors, Prefects, clerks and

Brotherhood take their cut I doubt there'll enough left
to pay for superior stone or marble.

'You know, Makri, this whole thing stinks. According to the Venerable Tresius the statue is important to
the Cloud Temple and the Star Temple because young
monks regard an Abbot without a good statue of Saint
Quatinius as about as much use as a eunuch in a
brothel. But I'm not sure if I believe that. After all, why
didn't Tresius think of that before he split off and set
up his own temple?'

'Tresius said he commissioned his own statue from
Drantaax. Ixial could have murdered Drantaax to
prevent him from finishing the statue – or to steal it for
himself.'

I'd forgotten that. Still sounds dubious though. 'I
guess it might be true. But the Venerable Tresius lied
about not meeting any other monks in the city. What
if he's really after the statue for his own temple and is
using me to locate it for him? Wouldn't be the first
time some criminal tried to use me as a means of finding something. Wouldn't be the tenth time in fact.'

'That's what you get for being good at finding
things. Still, you have the statue so I don't have to
worry too much about the details. Just make sure
Tresius doesn't steal it. What are you doing about
Grosex? I hear the trial starts in two days' time.'

This makes me frown. I suddenly notice the heat
again, and the dry, choking air. Every summer this
damned city is like this. You think it can't possibly get
any hotter, then it does. Two stals flop down on the
window sill outside, too exhausted to fly any further. I

glare at them moodily. I'm not fond of them.

'I was hoping Astrath could pick up the killer's aura if I found the statue but now it's been in the magic space that won't work. Which brings me back to the mundane matter of looking for witnesses. I need to speak to Drantaax's wife. Whatever she knows might be enough to fit together with what Tresius says and provide evidence against Ixial the Seer.'

It's puzzling that Calia hasn't appeared yet. It's not so easy for a person to hide in this city unless they are well versed in covering their tracks. I can't imagine that she would be. But with no relatives apart from her brother and no friends that anyone knows of, where would she go? Lodging houses cost money. Anyway, the Guards have been checking them.

'I must speak to her. Maybe she knows who the murderer was and she's scared to come forward.'

'Maybe she knows who the murderer was so the murderer thought he'd better kill her as well,' suggests Makri, which, I have to admit, is a possibility. But the picture in the kuriya pool gave me the impression she was alive. Alive in a white villa. There are a lot of white villas in Thamlin.

Whoever murdered Drantaax must have had the magic purse ready to put the statue in, which does make it fairly certain that they murdered Thalius first. My head starts to swim. I can feel myself getting involved in too many cases at once, a bad habit of mine.

'So don't ask me about the dolphins. I don't have time to even think about them. And keep Quen out of my sight. The Brotherhood are stepping up their search. We better just hope Astrath Triple Moon really can boost the bafflement spell and keep her hidden. We might be able to move her in a day or two when the heat's off.'

Makri has heard that the Innkeepers Guild has been complaining in high places about the Guards' failure to locate the killer of the landlord.

'They're demanding that the Abode of Justice assigns a higher-grade Sorcerer to the case.'

'Great. Where did you hear that?'

'Association of Gentlewomen. We have a member who works as a cook in the Abode of Justice.'

I growl. Innkeepers don't have a particularly high social status in Turai but their guild is surprisingly well connected. Not so surprising, I guess. Even Praetors and Senators like to go out for a drink every now and then. And as the Innkeepers Guild shares various business interests with the Brotherhood and the Society of Friends, it's not really safe to meddle with them. If the Civil Guard gets going on this as well I'm in deep trouble.

Then there's the monks. Maybe Sarin the Merciless too. A lesser man might go to pieces. I go downstairs for a helping of Tanrose's stew and some more beer. If I'm going to find Drantaax's wife, I'll need plenty of energy.

Makri isn't due to work till this evening. She was planning to spend the afternoon practising a speech for her rhetoric class. This has been causing some mirth around the Avenging Axe, with heartless individuals, like me for instance, pointing out that while Makri's voice might be excellent for bellowing death threats across a gladiatorial arena, it doesn't seem all that suitable for the fine art of oratory. Makri ignores the mockery, but agrees to postpone her practice and come out with me, saying that she's been short of activity of late, and saving me from a band of deadly warrior monks might be good exercise.

I strap on my sword and stick a knife in the small scabbard concealed at the back of my waistband. Makri wears both her swords, more or less hidden under her cloak, and slips a long knife into each of her boots. As usual, she is not entirely comfortable without her axe, but it's too conspicuous. There is no legal reason why a woman can't walk around Turai carrying an axe, but it isn't exactly an everyday sight. A fully armed Makri – lithe, strong, and a blade sticking out in every direction – presents a very worrying sight for the Civil Guard. She tends to get stopped and questioned, which is inconvenient when we're on a case. Also, we get refused entry to high-class establishments.

She's still grumbling as we head out through the potholes, fish heads and assorted debris of Quintessence Street.

'You never know when you'll need your axe. Once, in the slave pits, I was fighting four Orcs and my first sword broke and then my other sword got stuck in the second Orc's rib cage. I had to finish off the other two with my knife and when I stabbed the last one my knife blade broke as well. I mean, bad luck, or what? Actually, it might have been sorcery because by this

time I was supreme champion and some of the Orc
Lords were getting jealous of my success and the way I
kept killing their gladiators. So, right then, just when I
didn't have a weapon, they threw in this enormous
Troll carrying a nine-foot spear and a club the size of a
Human. So that just goes to show.'

'Goes to show what?'

'That you should never be without your axe.'

'We'll just have to hope we don't meet a giant Troll
at the end of Quintessence Street. What happened?
Did you kill the Troll with your bare hands?'

'No. Trolls are too strong for that. I vaulted up the
wall to the Orc Lord's gallery. His chief bodyguard ran
in front of me so I took his sword off him, stabbed him
with it, and leaped back into the arena. After all this
the Troll was confused and I was able to hack him to
pieces. By now the Orc Lord was angry I'd killed his
chief bodyguard, so all the rest of his bodyguards
started leaping down into the arena, eight of them, all
in chainmail. It was a pretty close thing for a while,
what with eight of them chasing me around and me
with only one sword to defend myself. But after I disposed of a couple I managed to pick up another sword
and once I had one in each hand I just mowed them
down. Should have seen the crowd. They were going
completely berserk. I had the longest standing ovation
ever granted to a gladiator.'

I glance sideways at Makri. When she arrived in
Turai about a year ago one of her notable features was
her inability to lie. But she's been learning recently,
mainly from me.

'Is that story true? Or are you just practising for your speech at the rhetoric class?'

'Of course it's true. Why wouldn't it be? You think I can't defeat thirteen Orcs and a Troll? Now you mention it, though, it would make a good speech.'

'What subject are you meant to be talking about?'

'Living peacefully in a violent world.'

'Best of luck.'

'I'll need it. Last rhetoric exam, I didn't do very well at all.'

We take a landus up through town. The streets are hot as Orcish hell and as the day wears on it doesn't get any cooler. I call in on the small room in a tenement where Grosex lived on his own. No one in the building seems to know anything about him. The neighbours hardly saw him and don't think he's got any relations anywhere. The neighbours also hope that he'll be hanged. After all, he's just murdered our most famous artist.

I search his room, with no results. Nothing of interest, criminal or otherwise. Just a shabby little room for an apprentice who can't afford anything better. The floor boards are bare. The walls are stained with candle smoke. From upstairs come the screams of a misbehaving child and the hopeless shrieks of an enraged mother. I shudder.

'Lets get out of here. It's depressing me.'

Poor Grosex. No friends or relations. Living in that miserable little room on his own. I can see he might have enjoyed some diversion in the shape of Drantaax's wife.

We head north. We're on our way to see Lisutaris, Mistress of the Sky. Lisutaris is a powerful Sorcerer, and unconnected with any of the official bodies in Turai. She has a large independent income so she doesn't have to work at the Abode of Justice or the Palace, or draw up horoscopes and lucky charms for private citizens. This is just as well, as Lisutaris smokes raw thazis through a waterpipe all day and is permanently stoned.

I helped her out a few months ago so she might be willing to help me now though I'm not counting on it. Makri is more hopeful. They've met at a few Association of Gentlewomen meetings and the Sorcerer has appeared friendly enough, unlike some other well-born women Makri could name. Even the Association of Gentlewomen is not without its share of prejudice against anyone with Orc blood. Several Senator's wives have refused to sit in the same room as her.

Our landus comes to a halt in a narrow street as a large cart full of vegetables stops in front of us. Our driver shouts some abuse to no effect. The other driver seems to have disappeared and the vegetable cart stays where it is. We look round as our driver considers the tricky option of reversing his horse and cart down the narrow street. Standing behind us are five red-robed monks who by this simple manoeuvre have now cornered us. They stare at us quite calmly. The one in front, a small individual with boyish features, waves his hand in greeting. Makri and I leap down from the landus to confront them.

'What do you want?' I demand.

'The statue of Saint Quatinius,' says the small monk, quite placidly. I notice that he is not sweating in the heat, like the rest of the population.

'What's that got to do with me?'

'We know that you have it.'

My temper starts to boil. Who does he think he is, hijacking my landus when I'm out on a case? I tell him to go to hell. He doesn't. Instead he just stands there placidly, which annoys me more than ever. I try and shove him out of the way but he somehow avoids my push. I lose my temper completely and throw a punch at his annoyingly peaceful face.

He dodges it. And then throws a punch, not at me, but at the thick plank of wood at the rear of the landus. To my astonishment the small man's fist snaps it in two, sending splinters into the air.

'Where is the statue?' he repeats.

I try to draw my sword but before it's out of its scabbard he hits me and I fly backwards into the landus. A spar catches me in the ribs and I tumble on to the ground, gasping for breath.

Makri figures this is enough provocation for anyone and draws her swords. The monks take out some curiously shaped knives, each with long guards curving out from their handles, which they use to deflect Makri's blade. And they do indeed block her blade, something I've never seen before. They move with lightning speed, so that Makri is quickly encircled. Despite landing a cut on one opponent's shoulder, she is brought down by a kick from behind that she has no

room to avoid. She's on her feet in an instant, landing
a good kick of her own before thrusting herself against
the nearest wall so they can't get behind her. Standing
with her twin swords forming an impenetrable guard,
she waits for them to come on to her.

I raise myself off the ground and walk a few
yards so Makri is not in my way. I have my own
sword in my hand and for all their fighting skill I'll
fight five people with Makri at my side any day. But
right now I don't have the time and it's too hot. So I
let go with the sleep spell. The five monks crumple
instantly to the floor.

Makri looks round angrily at me – I know she will
regard this magic as a dishonourable way of dealing
with opponents – but she doesn't protest. She's not
used to meeting anyone who can land a kick on her
and is looking puzzled.

Our landus driver is looking more than puzzled.
He's quaking in his seat.

I ask him if he can clear the vegetable wagon from
in front of us. He does this readily enough, leaping on
the horse and taking the reins while I search the
monks. I don't find a thing. They don't even have any
pockets and none of them is carrying a bag. Just their
curious knives. Makri takes all five for her collection.

The way is now clear. There are only a few minutes
left till the warrior monks wake up. Less, if they have
strong constitutions, which they probably do. We set
off with as much speed as is possible through the
crowded streets.

Makri's face is dark with fury.

'You annoyed because I put them to sleep?'

She shakes her head.

'No. I'm annoyed that I underestimated them. I can't believe I let someone kick me from behind.'

She lapses into gloomy silence for the rest of the journey.

'Don't worry about it,' I tell her. 'No doubt you'll get to meet them again soon. There'll be plenty of opportunity to kick them back.'

CHAPTER
NINE

Lisutaris, Mistress of the Sky, is about the same age as me but much better preserved. I suspect that female Sorcerers have their own arcane beauty secrets to fight the ravages of time, but they've never shared them with me. She has long fair hair, woven in braids, which are piled on her head before trailing down her back. It's all held in place by a sort of tiara, silver, studded with pearls, in a style quite common among aristocratic women.

Well-born Turanian women spend much time and effort on their hair. Makri, with her vast unruly mane, affects some scorn at this. There is no denying, though, that on Lisutaris it is quite fetching, as is her rainbow cloak, which is of a finer cut and cloth than the standard Sorcerer's garment.

The last time I was here howling mobs were outside trying to burn the villa down, and wounded Sorcerers lay all over the floor. Lisutaris was lying on the floor as well, but her stupor was because of thazis rather than injury. I found a spell in her workroom for making the plants grow faster, which I suppose goes some way to explain why Lisutaris spends most of her time attached to a large waterpipe inhaling the fumes from her specially grown private supply.

Thazis is still illegal in Turai. Only six or so years ago the Civil Guards were hot on tracking down offenders, if only to gather enough of the substance for themselves to smoke in private. Senators used to make impassioned speeches denouncing its use and blaming it for the moral decay that was gripping the nation's youth. Since dwa swept the city, no one bothers any more. Most people smoke thazis as a mild relaxant and antidote to their worries, though few are so enthusiastic and overindulgent as Lisutaris. She is notorious in certain circles for inventing a new kind of waterpipe. It could be worse. At least she isn't a dwa addict. That's turning out to be quite a popular occupation among the city's Sorcerers.

We are greeted hospitably enough when we arrive. A servant leads us through long corridors to a large airy room with green and gold Elvish tapestries on the walls and plants of all kinds surrounding a bay window overlooking the extensive gardens. Everyone has extensive gardens in Thamlin, and a team of gardeners on the payroll. If you don't, you lose status. Another servant brings us wine and announces that Lisutaris will be down presently.

From what I've seen of the villa, Lisutaris has followed the current Thamlin fashion of bringing in an interior designer, probably from Attical. I can remember when Sorcerers' houses were perpetually strewn with sorcerous junk which no amount of servants could keep entirely clean, but a fashionable woman such as Lisutaris would no longer be satisfied with that. Since Turai's gold mines started bringing in the wealth, everyone in Thamlin is much more concerned with style. Senators used to gain status from their prowess on the battlefield. Now they attain it through modish living rooms and exquisitely tended gardens. I don't approve of this, but I'm old-fashioned.

I'm not quite sure how to approach Lisutaris with my requests. It is not the done thing to apply to a Sorcerer for help in locating people, unless the Sorcerer actually hires himself out for that sort of thing, which very few do. Apart from odd outcasts like myself, who never finished his training, and Astrath Triple Moon, who is now in disgrace, Sorcerers in Turai don't go in for much private enterprise. They either work for the King or the Consul or follow the standard lifestyle of the idle upper-class citizen who doesn't have to work at anything. Investigation is deemed to be below them, a job best left to the Civil Guards. Or me. Like the rest of the population, Sorcerers are very conscious of their social standing.

The brief wait for Lisutaris to appear turns into a long one. My patience quickly wears thin. The wine is excellent, but I don't have the time to enjoy it. Makri is still brooding about letting someone land a kick on her, and she sits stiffly in her chair.

'Lighten up, Makri. Just because you're number one chariot when it comes to fighting doesn't mean you have to be invincible. There were five of them and they're all specially trained. Some of these monks spend their whole lives in monasteries, doing nothing else expect fighting and praying.'

'Well, they'll have something to pray about next time we meet,' says Makri. She mutters a few dark threats about what she has in store for them.

Lisutaris arrives eventually, a faraway look in her eyes. A servant leads her to a chair trying to conceal the fact that he's actually holding her upright. I sigh. What is it about being a Sorcerer that makes these people indulge to such an excess?

'Can I bring you anything?' enquires the servant.

I notice my goblet is empty. 'Another bottle of wine if you don't mind.'

Lisutaris eventually focuses her eyes. When she sees Makri she smiles in recognition.

'Hello . . .?'

'Makri.'

'Hello, Makri.'

The Sorcerer looks at me. I can tell she doesn't remember me. I remind her of the riot.

'I was the one who slapped you.'

That didn't sound quite right.

'To bring you round. To put out the fire.'

She gazes at me vacantly.

'And then I fought off the crowd that was trying to kill us. Well, me and Hanama the Assassin did. Praetor Cicerius later described it as a heroic effort.'

Lisutaris continues to look vacant. 'My memories of that day are a little hazy. So much happened, with the fire and the riots, I just . . .'

Her voice trails off and her eyes drift to her Elvish tapestries. Lisutaris is laden with pale silver jewellery of Elvish design and she plays absently with one of the many slender bangles that adorn her wrists. We sit in silence as the Sorcerer drifts off in whatever thazis-fuelled dream she has found in the tapestries. As an experienced and reputable Sorcerer, Lisutaris, Mistress of the Sky, will have spent a fair amount of time among the Elves. Our Sorcerers always visit the Southern Islands when they are young, to study and learn.

I've been to the Southern Islands myself, which few other Turanian citizens can claim. Very beautiful. Not much crime. They have good wine, but beer is hard to find. Lisutaris carries on gazing at the tapestries and I start to feel a little awkward and somewhat annoyed. I saved this woman's life a few months ago. I don't especially care that she's forgotten, but it makes asking her for a favour more difficult. I'm about to do it anyway when Makri leaps in ahead of me.

'Can you help us find someone?' she asks.

The Mistress of the Sky withdraws her gaze from her tapestries and looks at Makri, surprised. Makri, of course, does not realise that it is a rude question.

'Look for someone?'

A trace of annoyance flickers over the Sorcerer's face. For a second I think she's going to throw us out. Then she shrugs, and smiles.

'If you wish. Who are you looking for?'

I let Makri do the explaining. I'm interested to learn that their acquaintance in the Association of Gentle-women is sufficient reason to break a social taboo. The Association is going to land itself in hot water with the King and the Church one day.

Lisutaris, Mistress of the Sky, reaches languidly for

a silk bell rope and summons a servant. She tells him to bring her some kuriya. He departs, soon returning with a golden saucer on a silver tray with a small gold bottle beside it. He places a small table before Lisutaris and puts the tray down where she can reach it.

Lisutaris sips some wine before reaching over to pour the black kuriya from the bottle into the saucer. Without any preparation at all, she waves her hand over the liquid. Within seconds a picture starts to appear.

I'm envious of her power. It takes me a long time to get myself into the required mental state to summon up a picture yet she can do it instantly, even when she's stoned. I should have studied more.

'Is this the house you mean?'

I study the picture. It is. Lisutaris concentrates for a few moments.

'It belongs to a man called Osicius. It's situated near to the fountain that stands outside the southern wall of the Palace.'

I thank Lisutaris profusely. She glances back into the dark pool.

'I see that Osicius has been going through some troubles recently. The aura of the house is disturbed. I also see that he is known by another name.'

For the first time she looks as if she is straining. 'Akial?' she says finally. 'Or Exil perhaps?'

'Not Ixial surely?' I say, quite loudly. 'Ixial the Seer?'

'That's right. Ixial the Seer. Well, he can't see me.'

And with that the mighty Sorceress gets a very inappropriate fit of the giggles and starts rolling around in her chair in hysterics. The picture fades from the kuriya pool. While I wonder at the very unexpected discovery that Drantaax's wife is concealed in the town house of Ixial the Seer, Lisutaris keeps right on laughing, interspersed with the odd burst of 'He can't see me', which seems to strike her as the funniest thing in the world.

She pulls the bell rope and orders the servant to bring her waterpipe. She offers to share some thazis with us. Makri is keen to try the waterpipe. I whisper to her that she'll look silly if five hostile warrior monks appear while she is laughing uncontrollably.

Makri's eyes harden at the thought and she refuses the offer. We thank Lisutaris, Mistress of the Sky, and take our leave. Outside we hail a landus and head on up to the south side of the Palace. Behind us Lisutaris is still finding things very amusing.

'Is she like that at your A.G. meetings?' I ask Makri.

'I cannot tell anyone anything about our meetings,' Makri replies.

'I know.'

We ride on.

'Actually she's worse,' says Makri. 'I'm surprised to see she's such a good Sorcerer. That was good sorcery, wasn't it?'

'Certainly was. I couldn't get pictures like that in the kuriya pool if I meditated for a month. Lisutaris is as decadent as the rest of our upper classes but she's sharp as an Elf's ear when it comes to magic. Good wine cellar too. Next time you run into her at a meeting see if she'll invite us to dinner. She might bring out the Elvish vintages. Incidentally, where do you hold your meetings?'

'I'm not meant to say.'

'You know that Archbishop Xerius made a speech to the Senate last week in which he roundly condemned the Association of Gentlewomen as a wicked and ungodly organisation?'

Makri says something rude about the Archbishop.

A few important people ride past in fancy carriages, but the streets are far quieter here than elsewhere. Far cleaner as well. Even the stals look better fed. Makri wonders out loud why Ixial the Seer, Abbot of a monastery in the mountains, would have a villa in Thamlin. It's a good question. And why has Calia fled there?

The villa is precisely where Lisutaris said it would be. We ride past without stopping. There's nothing to see. No one in sight, not even a gardener. No sign of anyone from the Securitus Guild either. It's quite common for these villas to be protected by their own private Guards but this one doesn't seem to be.

I ask the driver to drop us off some way past. Makri and I leave the main street and enter a park which I think leads to the back of the villa's garden. After some uncomfortable scrambling over thorns and bushes, we find ourselves confronted by a wall eight feet high topped with metal spikes.

'Here we are. The house is on the other side of this wall.'

'What are we going to do?'

'Take a look.'

The heat is still oppressive but I feel sharp. I become

frustrated when things get too complicated but when it comes down to the basics of investigation – like sticking my head over a wall and taking a good look – I feel in control.

The park was busy with nannies and tutors taking their young charges for walks and young Army Captains meeting chaperoned young ladies, but we've come far enough into the wooded area at the edge so that no one can see us. Makri offers to give me a boost up the wall, but I decide against giving her an opportunity to criticise me about my weight and stick a convenient log where I can stand on it. This gives me just enough height to see over.

'No one in sight,' I whisper. 'Let's go.'

Makri is looking dubious. 'Are you sure?'

'Of course. What's wrong?'

'I don't know. I suppose I'm just not used to climbing over other people's walls.

I was forgetting. Makri is dauntless in battle but she isn't used to the nitty-gritty of investigating such as sneaking round places you're not meant to be. I reassure her that I do this sort of thing all the time then lay my cloak over the metal spikes and haul myself over the wall. I drop down gently and slip behind a tree, where Makri joins me. There is still no one in sight. The light is fading as the sun sinks over the roof of the Palace in the distance, sending brilliant rays shooting from its golden towers.

'Are we going inside the villa? What do we say if someone catches us?'

'We'll just make some excuse. I always think of

something. And keep your swords in their scabbards.
If you kill anyone it'll just make things more complicated.'

Keeping low, we head from tree to tree, taking cover
and watching as we make the long trek towards the
villa.

'Big garden,' whispers Makri.

'They always are in Thamlin. Mine was huge.
Further than I could walk.'

The night comes quickly. Only one of the moons is
in the sky, low down to the east, and it casts little light
into the grounds.

Near the villa a large clump of bushes makes excellent cover and we crouch in the undergrowth before
making our final approach to the house. It is now
dark, but no lights burn inside. Very strange. Even if
the owner was away there would always be servants
left to take care of things. I feel some slight unease. If
everyone inside is dead I'd as soon it wasn't me that
found them. Such things happen to me way too often
and the Guards always give me a hard time about it.
'Dead Body Thraxas' they call me.

Suddenly the back door opens and figures emerge
carrying candles. They walk in silence. I strain my
eyes in the dim light to make out what's happening.
They're carrying something. It looks like a corpse.
Dead Body Thraxas strikes again. I go tense, wondering what I've stumbled into. They proceed towards us
in silence. Four figures, carrying another.

'Monks,' whispers Makri.

She's right. Monks with shaved heads. I can't

distinguish the colour of their cloaks. They approach. The figure they're carrying starts to show signs of life as the monks carefully lower him on to the ground where he kneels as if in meditation. Eventually the other monks kneel in front of the figure they have deposited, and stare at him by the dim candlelight. From their reverential attitude I guess that this must be Ixial the Seer.

My eyes start to adjust. There is someone else beside him. Not a monk. Too much hair. It's a young woman. Calia, I presume.

Ixial holds up his hand and seems about to speak. Something catches his attention and he pauses. He swivels his head towards us.

'Who is there?' he demands.

We freeze. I'd swear he couldn't see us here in the bushes, in the darkness.

'Come out,' he orders. 'You cannot hide from Ixial the Seer.'

'Fine,' I say, stepping out into the open. 'It was getting cramped in there anyway. You've got sharp eyes. But then I guess you would have, Ixial the Seer.'

The four attendant monks rise swiftly to stand between me and their leader.

'What do you want?' demands Ixial. 'And what is the meaning of entering into this garden uninvited?'

There's something odd about the way he's sitting. It's almost as if the woman beside him is actually supporting him. My first thought is that he is yet another dwa enthusiast but his voice seems too clear and firm.

'What do I want? Some conversation with the lady, mainly. About Grosex. One-time apprentice to the lady's recently departed husband Drantaax, and now languishing in prison awaiting a swift trial and execution. And after that I might like a few words with you about why your monks have been following me around the city, burgling my rooms and attacking me in alleyways.'

Several more monks emerge from the house and advance in the gloom to stand close behind Ixial. I wonder how many are in the house. I've used up the sleep spell and I'm not sure how many warrior monks Makri and I can handle at once.

Ixial starts to speak but halts, giving the faintest of groans. His face contorts. He is obviously in some pain and is fighting to control it. His followers turn their heads in concern. This is one sick Abbot. As Ixial slumps forward, Calia takes a small bottle from her bag and starts dabbing his lips and forehead with some liquid. None of the monks seems to have any idea what to do. They are all young, and I sense that they're frightened by their leader's distress. I step forward, brushing the monks aside.

'What's the matter with him?'

Calia looks up at me with despair in her eyes. No one tries to prevent me as I take a candle and reach down to move the blanket which covers his legs. His legs are a mess, twisted and broken. Each is protected by splints and bandages but blood oozes out from gaps everywhere and where the skin shows through it is black and putrid. If gangrene hasn't set in already, it isn't far away. I'd say that Ixial the Seer has about twenty-four hours to live, maybe less.

'We're waiting for the healers to arrive,' says Calia. Her voice is desperate, almost without hope. No healer is gong to save Ixial. So twisted and broken are his legs that I assume only his willpower and rigorous training have kept him alive this long. With injuries like that most people would have given up and died by now.

'What happened?'

Calia doesn't answer. I look down at Ixial. He opens his eyes for a moment. He struggles briefly with the pain then his head lolls forward as he loses consciousness.

More lights appear in the house as the healers arrive. Two women, each with the green canvas bags commonly used for carrying medicine, are led into the gardens, along with a man in a flowing robe. An apothecary, a herbalist and a healer. Good luck to them.

I withdraw to Makri's hiding place in the shadows. The monks are gathered in a circle around their leader as the doctors examine him.

'No chance,' I mutter. 'They should have brought an undertaker. It would have saved time.'

Makri is wary of the monks. Only hours ago they

were trailing us through the city. Now they seem too concerned with their leader's plight to bother about us.

'I need to speak to Calia. Dying Abbot or not, I'm here to clear Grosex.'

Oil lamps have been lit for the healers. While they go about their business Calia stands to one side in the shadows, ignored by the monks.

'She doesn't look in a mood to talk,' says Makri.

'I never let that bother me.'

'You want me to come?'

'Yes. She might feel better with another woman around.'

'Even an Orc with pointed ears?'

'I'm sure I never called you that.'

We circumnavigate the healers and the monks.

'I need to talk to you.'

'Not now,' says Calia.

I can see that she deserved her reputation as a Twelve Seas beauty but I can also see that she's been under immense strain. Her husband was killed only a few days ago. But I get the impression that he isn't uppermost in her mind.

'It has to be now. Unless you want Grosex to hang.'

She looks up sharply. 'Grosex? Hang? Why?'

'For murdering Drantaax, of course.'

'That's ridiculous. He wouldn't have killed Drantaax.'

'That's not what you said when you found Grosex standing over the body. I heard you were screaming out he'd stabbed him.'

Calia brushes this off. 'I wasn't thinking clearly. Who would be? I don't know who killed my husband, but I'm sure it wasn't the apprentice. He was far too loyal.'

'It was his knife.'

'Someone else must have used it.'

'The Guards don't think so.' I ask her who did and she says she doesn't know. I don't think I believe her.

'Tell me what's going on. What happened at the workshop? And why did you run here? What's your connection with Ixial?'

This gets no response.

'You'll feel better if you talk about it,' I add. I often find this a useful line, but it doesn't work for Calia. I change tack.

'What happened to Ixial?'

'They attacked while he was meditating.'

'Who did?'

'Tresius. The Cloud Temple. They sneaked up on him while he was praying and threw him from the walls.'

'What happened to his seeing powers?'

'Ixial is a religious man,' retorts Calia. 'He does not distract himself with seeing while he is praying.'

I see. That's not the way Tresius told it. According to Calia, Tresius and his followers had been apprehended trying to steal the monastery's statue before they departed in disgrace. The statue had tumbled to its destruction from the walls. But Tresius had later returned with the intention of killing Ixial and stealing his followers. During this altercation the Cloud

Temple was repulsed but Ixial, taken by surprise, was himself tumbled from the walls, suffering the terrible injuries he now has.

'The monks brought him to the city to try and save his life.'

The despair on her face shows quite clearly she knows it's hopeless. Any normal man would have died by now. Every healer, herbalist and apothecary in Turai isn't going to be able to put Ixial's twisted and broken legs back together. Nor could they cure the gangrene that'll kill him if loss of blood doesn't do so first. Even Sorcerers are powerless against gangrene.

Calia is more forthcoming. She tells us that she'd been involved with Ixial a decade ago when he was nothing more than a poor young student living in a garret in Twelve Seas, reading scrolls of philosophy by candlelight. She was in love with him then, and still is. When he went off into the wilderness to take up the life of a monk, she'd despaired of ever being happy again. Eventually she ended up marrying Drantaax, having no better prospects and parents keen to get their hands on the dowry from a famous and wealthy sculptor.

She tells me she spent ten years with Drantaax during which time her life was comfortable but desperately dull. And so it might have remained, had she not received a message from Ixial the Seer asking her to meet him at a villa in Thamlin.

She went to meet him. And started an affair, I imagine, though she doesn't come right out and say it.

This all raises some interesting questions. How did

an Abbot of a mountain monastery find the money to buy a large villa in Thamlin, for instance? And what was he doing with it anyway? Warrior monks live in harsh conditions, training their minds and bodies with rigorous exercise. I don't think they make exceptions for their Abbots. They're not meant to adopt false names, pretend to be aristocrats and hang around in villas in wealthy parts of town. I don't think they're meant to have affairs with married ex-lovers either, although different sects adopt different views on celibacy and such like. But I have to leave these questions for now, and concentrate on Grosex. Now that Calia has opened up a little, she tells me what she knows. Simply put, she arrived in the workshop to find Grosex standing over Drantaax's body and the statue gone.

That's the same story as the Guards so far.

'Why did you flee?'

'I panicked. I knew there were stories about me having an affair. People thought I'd been seeing Grosex when really I had been seeing Ixial. I thought the Guards would accuse me of killing my husband so Grosex could have his business. So I fled. I didn't know they'd suspect Grosex. I liked him. I didn't mean to bring him any harm, but I had to get away.'

'Sounds like you were glad of the chance.'

'So what if I was?'

She puts a great deal of feeling into that. Maybe it's unbearable being married to a busy sculptor.

'You don't sound shattered with grief about his murder.'

'I'm sad. I've got other things to be sadder about.'

'What happened to the statue?'

She claims not to know. If she is aware of the goings-on with the magic purse, she's not letting on. I point out to her that the statue thief must surely be the murderer, and Ixial and the Star Temple were currently minus one statue. Which does make them a strong suspect.

She shakes her head. 'Ixial would not have harmed my husband. Why would he? And anyway, when Drantaax's statue went missing Ixial was already close to death. It's taken his monks four days to transport him from the mountains to the city.'

'Injured or not, he was still giving out orders, because his monks have been searching the city. Searching my rooms anyway.'

'I know nothing of that.'

Ixial calls out in pain. Calia hurries over to him. I look at the young monks, trying to gauge their reaction to her. Are they aware of her relationship with their leader, or has he deceived them with some story? I see no signs of disapproval on their faces.

I turn to Makri. 'What do you make of it?'

'I'm completely confused,' she replies. 'Who did kill Drantaax, then? And who stole the statue and put it in the magic purse?'

I admit that I don't know.

'I don't understand that woman,' continues Makri. 'If she didn't want to marry Drantaax, then why did she? She didn't need a husband. She could've got a job in Minarixa's bakery.'

'I don't think Calia is the type to spend her days in a bakery.'

The healing goes on by the light of the lamps. Ixial drifts in and out of consciousness. Finally he lapses into a deep sleep, or maybe a deep coma. The healer, the herbalist and the apothecarist exchange glances, which are not hard to interpret. Ixial will be handing in his toga pretty soon. Several of the younger monks have tears in their eyes. If I was a man of sensitivity I'd leave them all to their grief. But I'm not. I grab the sleeve of one monk whom I think I recognise as one of the burglars at my office.

'Why did you think I had the statue?'

He yanks his sleeve away and hurries off to join his fellows. I question another with similar results.

'You're not going to learn anything more here, Thraxas,' says Makri. 'They're all too worried about Ixial. I feel kind of annoyed really. They owe me a fight.'

As if on cue the silent garden suddenly erupts. Yellow-clad monks pour over the walls, and they haven't come to talk about consubstantiality. They charge towards the monks of the Star Temple yelling war cries and waving short sticks and curious knives. The Star Temple monks react quickly, forming a human shield around Ixial. More of their brothers hear the uproar and rush from the house. Soon eighty or so monks are battling away in the garden, punch-ing, kicking, and flying through the air in their now familiar acrobatic manner. It's quite a sight. Makri and I withdraw to the bushes to watch, slightly bewil-dered by this turn of events. I start to suspect that there may be no more reason behind any of this apart from the two Temples' hatred of each other. Maybe they just fight all the time anyway, and the statue is no more than a side issue.

'Interesting religious dispute,' I mutter to Makri as a monk bounces off a tree and crashes into the bush beside us. 'They should try it in the True Church. Certainly liven things up a bit.'

It's hard to be sure in the dim light, but I think I can see the Venerable Tresius in the thick of things. If it is him he's even better preserved for his age than I thought. I swear he leaps eight feet from the ground to hurtle over an opponent, kicking him as he does so, and lands behind another one whom he scythes to the ground with another kick to the legs. He finds himself surrounded by a group of red monks but leaps clear after sending two of them hurtling backwards into the pond.

Cries of anger and pain ring out from all sides as the monks surge this way and that. While some knives are in view most of the fighting is done empty-handed. Everyone seems to be doing their best to maintain the warrior monks' reputation as masters of unarmed combat. I wince as a pile-driving blow sends another young novice crashing into the bushes to lie unconscious at our feet.

'Should have kept your guard up,' murmurs Makri who, I suspect, is enjoying the spectacle.

'Should we join in?' she asks.

'Of course not. Why would we?'

'I don't know. I just thought maybe we should.'

'Just because there's a fight doesn't mean you have to get involved, Makri.'

'I suppose not. It just doesn't seem natural not to.'

The yellow-robed monks of the Cloud Temple seem to have the upper hand, mainly because of the presence of the Venerable Tresius who carries everyone before him. None of the young monks in red can stand up to his furious fighting technique. Bodies literally fly into the air in front of him as he smashes one young novice after another out of the way. He fights his way to the edge of Ixial's bodyguard and keeps right on going. His followers fan out and start to attack from all directions.

The healer, the herbalist and the apothecarist have wisely fled the scene but I think Calia is still by Ixial's side, ready to defend him to the last. The power of love, I reflect. I have to admire her for it.

The brothers of the Star Temple put up a desperate defence. They're brave and unflinching but Tresius is just too much for them, brushing them out of the way like a dragon going through a squadron of poorly paid mercenaries. I wonder if he intends to kill Ixial? As an Investigator, sworn to uphold the law, I should act to prevent such a serious crime being committed right under my nose, but it's not really my affair when it comes right down to it.

Suddenly I sense someone close to us in the bushes. So does Makri. We turn round as one to the place where a dark-shadowed figure has moved in silence. The figure notes our presence but pays us no more attention. He raises something I can't quite discern.

There's a sharp twang and a brief humming sound and the next thing I know one of the yellow monks cries out in pain and slumps to the ground. I recognise the humming sound. A crossbow. I don't need an introduction to know who the figure in the shadows is.

'Sarin the Merciless,' I whisper to Makri.

The crossbow is both powerful and unwieldy. It's good for defending a city or launching an assault from cover but not much used on the battlefield because of its slowness to load. But in less time than I've ever seen it done before, Sarin has another deadly bolt in the groove. She fires it off, killing another of the Cloud Temple monks. As their second man goes down the yellow monks start to realise that something is wrong and pause slightly in their attack, unsure of what's happening. Another bolt flies from the crossbow. Another monk goes down.

'In the bushes,' yells the Venerable Tresius, gesturing with his hand.

The interruption helps the Star Temple regroup and they re-form a solid defence around Ixial. Monks of the Cloud Temple are now running towards the bushes. I watch as Sarin the Merciless coolly loads another bolt into her weapon. This time she takes more careful aim. She fires at Tresius.

Tresius does something that is not humanly possible. He seizes the bolt out of the air before it hits him. I gasp in astonishment. A bolt from a crossbow has enough power at close range to go in through one wall and out through another. It's not possible to grab it out of the air in mid-flight. You can't even see it. And yet Tresius just did.

His followers reach the bushes. I step further back into the shadows. Sarin calmly fires a final bolt into the nearest of her attackers then engages the rest with an unarmed combat technique which matches theirs. Her boast that she'd spent four years studying in a monastery must have been true. She's up against three opponents and acquitting herself well, sending one spinning backwards, then circling round the other two, denying them an opportunity to attack.

Whistles sound in the distance. The Civil Guard has been alerted. You can't stage a large battle in Thamlin without the neighbours complaining, and when the neighbours complain in Thamlin, the Guards take notice. There are screams and yells and whistles and the sounds of horse-drawn wagons arriving at the front of the house. Seconds later men wearing the black tunics of the Civil Guard are swarming into the garden.

'Time to go.'

We depart swiftly, finding ourselves running towards the far wall in the company of various monks. I think I notice another figure in the shadows, a small figure, not a monk. Reminds me of someone, but I can't think who. By the time we're across the wall and into the park we're on our own.

'That was quite a night.'

'Great fight.'

We hurry away from the scene. Having once lived here I know my way around even in the dark. I lead us down a little-used lane between two villas till the sound of the uproar fades away. We now face a long walk home. Horse travel is forbidden in Turai at night. The night is still too hot to walk comfortably, and I realise I haven't eaten or drunk for some time.

'Did you learn enough to clear Grosex?' Makri enquires.

'I'm not sure. I'll need a while to sort it all out. Right now I need a beer. Why don't they have more taverns up here? First one we reach, I'm going in.'

It's well past midnight. As nightlife in this district is not particularly raucous, we don't find a tavern open until we're almost out of Thamlin and into Jade Temple Fields, which is a fraction more lively. Jade Temple Fields takes its name, naturally enough, from the old temple with jade columns built as a present from the Elves three hundred years ago after we helped them in a war with the Orcs. Turai sent the biggest contingent of ships with the fleet of the League of City-States and we crushed the Orcish Armada at the famous Battle of Dead Dragon Island. That put an end to Orcish sea power for a long time. Turai's great Navy was formidable in those days, despite our relatively small size. Not any more. We used to be an important member of the League of City-States. We still are in theory, but everyone knows the Army and Navy are not what they were.

The League isn't what it was, either. It's protected smaller city-states from the aggression of our larger neighbours like Nioj for the last four centuries but it's been falling apart for the past twenty years. Now we're in a permanent state of alert over the silver mines that border on our supposed ally Mattesh in the south. If we end up at war with them the League will disintegrate and Nioj will eat us all for breakfast.

Jade Temple Fields is home to government workers, lesser civil servants and the like. We finally find a tavern where the lights are still on. Makri looks at it suspiciously.

'It'll be fine,' I reassure her, and march in.

We're confronted at the door by a large individual wearing a green tunic signifying him as a member of the Securitus Guild, hired to keep out undesirables. Not like the Avenging Axe. Gurd will let anyone in.

The doorway is illuminated by a flaming torch. In the flickering firelight Makri's skin looks even redder than usual. The Guard is a mountainous individual. He stretches his arm out, preventing us from entering.

'No swords in here,' he grunts, looking at Makri. 'And no Orcs.'

So Makri, without any hesitation whatsoever, hauls off and punches him in the face. He crumples to the ground.

I stare at her. 'Couldn't we even have discussed it first?'

'What's to discuss? He insulted me.'

True enough. But I badly wanted a beer.

'We'll find another tavern,' says Makri.

The Guard is lying unconscious in the doorway. I'm tempted to hurdle the body and rush inside for a quick flagon of ale anyway, but decide against it. It'll only lead to trouble if he wakes up while I'm at the bar.

We trudge on through the hot night.

'I really think you ought to work on controlling your temper, Makri.'

'I'll start on it tomorrow. Good punch, wasn't it?'

Makri has cheered up and is no longer looking as miserable as a Niojan whore, which she has been ever since the monk kicked her. Which is quite probably why she punched the doorman. Just keen to have some unarmed combat practice in case she meets them again.

CHAPTER
ELEVEN

Next day I sleep late and wake up with sore legs and a nasty hangover. I struggle out of bed and make straight for my small store of lesada leaves. These come from the Elvish Islands and are very effective against hangovers. I acquired them from an Elf who hired me a couple of months ago. He turned out to be a treacherous criminal and ended up dead, but at least he left something useful behind.

Hanama the Assassin killed him and his companion, and the thought jogs my memory. That small dark figure I glimpsed in the gardens last night reminded me of Hanama. That would be all I need, the Assassins Guild mixing itself up in things.

The lesada leaf quickly starts to take effect. As the hangover recedes I realise I'm stiff all over. It was a long walk home last night, interrupted by a lengthy stay in a tavern in Kushni. No problems for Makri there. The tavern was so disreputable I doubt they'd have turned away the King of the Orcs provided he had a few gurans in his pocket.

The Kushni quarter in the centre of town is a crime-ridden, dwa-soaked collection of taverns, brothels and gambling dens run by and fought over by the Brotherhood and the Society of Friends and habituated by the assembled lowlife of Turai. I come here often in the course of my work. Makri, who doesn't have much spare time for socialising, isn't quite so familiar with it. I suspect she was taken by surprise by the potency of the alcohol served. She claimed she wasn't drunk but I swear it took her fifteen minutes to climb the outside stairs when we arrived home and she wouldn't have made it at all if I hadn't hauled her up the last flight myself.

So I'm slightly gratified when Makri crawls into my room about lunchtime and begs a lesada leaf from me. She's wrapped in an old blanket and looks like she has a bad dose of the plague. I don't mind Makri being number one chariot when it comes to fighting and she can be as sharp as an Elf's ear with her studies in philosophy and rhetoric, but I'd really take offence if she started outdrinking me.

Her hand shakes as she raises a goblet of water to her lips.

'You're looking as green as the leaf,' I comment cheerfully. 'I told you that mountain klee was too powerful for you. Needs a strong stomach like mine to take that beverage in.'

'What the hell was it made of?' groans Makri.

'Oh, grapes, yams, corn . . . Who knows? Up in the mountains they just distil whatever comes to hand.'

She shudders. 'Don't you feel bad?'

'Of course not. Take more than a couple of bottles of mountain klee to affect me. I was up bright and early for morning prayers.'

'Nonsense,' says Makri, wincing with the effort of

speaking. 'You just got to the lesada leaves first.'

Makri washes her leaf down with some difficulty then lies back on the couch with her arm covering her eyes.

'I don't think I can make that morning theology class.'

I clear some junk off my table. Makri uncovers her eyes and looks at me with some ire.

'Stop bustling around. I know you're just trying to show the drink didn't affect you. I'm going to kill Dandelion.'

'What?'

'I'm going to kill her. As soon as I feel better I'll run her through with my Orcish blade.'

Dandelion has apparently been droning on about the dolphins again. Makri, normally sympathetic, found it hard to take in her weakened state.

'Though I could do with the healing stone right now. I'm never going drinking in Kushni again.'

She lapses into mordant silence and waits for the leaf to do its work. Despite the heat of the morning she huddles miserably in her blanket and continues to look green. Poor Makri. I decide not to remind her that she actually sat on the lap of a young dwa dealer and attempted to kiss him before being thrown out the tavern. I'll save that one till she's stronger.

Downstairs Gurd and Tanrose are already at work. I study Tanrose's menu, selecting a few items for a hearty breakfast. I choose the fish. Tanrose cooks a fine plate of fish. I notice Gurd stiffening slightly as I order. Fish always puts him in a bad mood. The local fishmonger, quite a prosperous man by the standards of the neighbourhood, has had his eye on Tanrose for some time, and always gives her a good deal when it comes to buying his wares. This makes Gurd jealous. Poor old Barbarian. Having spent most of his life marching round the world fighting for anyone willing to pay him, he still can't get to grips with the idea of romance. He has got a crush on Tanrose that isn't getting any better. She doesn't mind this at all, but Gurd unfortunately can't quite bring himself to do anything about it. Too used to being a bachelor. Meanwhile he suffers like crazy whenever the fishmonger comes around and starts giving Tanrose big discounts.

By the time I've finished my breakfast Makri has appeared downstairs, bright-eyed and healthy.

'The leaves of the lesada tree,' she states, 'have miraculous powers. How many more do you have?'

'Not many. And they're almost impossible to get hold of in Turai. Next time I have an Elf for a client I'll ask for some in payment again.'

Makri points out that these weren't actually part of my payment from the last Elf.

'You just helped yourself after we found him dead.'

'Much the same thing.'

'I'm a bit hazy on the details of last night. Did we meet Sarin, or did I imagine it?'

'We met her. And she killed some monks with her crossbow. I've been trying to figure out what it all means. She's obviously on the side of the Star Temple. I presume she once trained under the tutelage of Ixial. I wonder if she killed Drantaax? It would be hard to prove because she's too smart to leave evidence lying around. Grosex goes on trial today. I finally got permission to see him, for what it's worth.'

'How come?'

'Deputy Consul Cicerius came back into town at last. He arranged it for me.'

I helped Cicerius's son out of trouble a few months back.

'That turned out to be a smart move,' says Makri. 'He's the first friend in a high place you've had in a long time.'

'That's true. Though I wouldn't count him a friend. Cicerius is too austere to actually have friends. Also, he probably remembers that I insulted him when I was drunk. But at least he'll ensure that my legal rights are upheld when it comes to court matters. And Grosex sure needs some help from somewhere. He's been assigned a public defendant, so if I don't dig something up they might as well take him out and hang him now.'

Makri gets herself outside of some fish. I take a lunchtime beer and consider the situation. I can't exactly interpret what's going on with the monks. Obviously the Venerable Tresius wasn't entirely straight with me. He neglected to mention that his followers had mortally wounded Ixial the Seer for one thing. So where does that leave me? I still have the purse with the statue in it. Tresius has hired me to find it. Maybe it doesn't matter exactly who did what to whom as far as the monks are concerned. I guess I'll pick up the fee for that anyway.

I'm troubled by meeting Sarin, though. She is a dangerous woman, and no mistake. If Ixial dies I imagine the Star Temple will disband and the monks will go over to the Cloud Temple. But if that doesn't happen and the red monks come looking for the statue again, I'll have Sarin to deal with as well. And then there's Thalius Green Eye. Who killed him? He was murdered with a crossbow which makes Sarin the obvious suspect, but it's not impossible that someone else might be trying to cover their tracks.

'Well, I reckon I've narrowed down the suspects for killing Drantaax to the monks of the Star Temple, the monks of the Cloud Temple, his wife Calia, Sarin the Merciless, and the domestic staff. Maybe a hundred people all told. If Grosex can keep from getting hanged for another year or two, I might whittle it down to single figures.'

Palax and Kaby have been out early busking with a mandolin and a flute. They look as peculiar as ever. Not only do they wear the strangest collection of bright and ragged clothes ever seen in Turai, their hair practically defies description. They grow it long and thick and dye it with food colouring and herbs into bright colours quite unsuitable for a person's head. To make things worse they're also well advanced in the matter of piercings. Many people in Turai sport pierced ears – in some guilds it's a mark of rank – but young Palax and Kaby, for some unfathomable reason, have rings through their noses and lips. Most shockingly, they wear rings through their eyebrows too, a style never before seen in the lands of Humans, and possibly too bizarre even for an Orcish whorehouse. I suppose street entertainers are allowed to be a little odd. Having grown up in an Orcish slave pen, Makri is lacking in public decorum, and asked them to pierce her nose a few months ago. Appalling behaviour, as I immediately pointed out to her, and hardly the sort of attitude she should adopt if she ever wants to get into the Imperial University. As the University already has enough reasons not to accept her, there seems no reason to provide them with another one. But Makri likes the ring through her nose, and figures the University will be able to get used to it.

The young musicians sit down wearily at a table.

'There's a Sorcerer outside,' says Kaby.

'Doing what?'

'Looking puzzled.'

'He's with that new Brotherhood boss, Casax.'

Bad news. I go to the door and look. As reported, there is a Sorcerer outside, looking puzzled. He's young, and while his rainbow cloak distinguishes him as a fully qualified Sorcerer, I don't recognise him so he probably hasn't been qualified for long. Beside him are Casax, Karlox and a few other Brotherhood men, all looking expectantly at the Sorcerer.

Casax spots me and strides across the dusty road towards me.

I greet him civilly. He greets me with an icy stare.

'We're looking for Quen.'

'Who?'

'The whore that burned down the Boar's Head.'

'I expect she's left the city by now.'

'Not according to Orius Fire Tamer, she hasn't. He reckons she's still around here somewhere.'

I study the young Sorcerer.

'Orius Fire Tamer? He's new, isn't he? Must've qualified recently. You know, Casax, you can't really trust such a young Sorcerer. He comes fresh out of his apprenticeship thinking he knows everything, but it takes a while to adjust to the ways of a city like Turai. Sure, he's followed Quen's aura this far, but so what? Everyone knows she was around here somewhere. When everyone's talking about someone it can create a false aura. Enough to confuse a young man just starting out in business. Quen is long gone by now. If you want to trace her you'll have to hire a more experienced man. Or woman. Lisutaris, Mistress of the Sky, is very good, so I hear.'

Casax isn't given to blustering. He looks at me quite coolly and informs me that the Brotherhood only tolerate my presence in the area because I never really get in their way. But if he finds I've got anything to do with hiding Quen then he'll be down on me like a bad spell.

'You'd better make sure you have another city to go to, and get there fast.'

'I'll bear it in mind. Maybe Deputy Consul Cicerius could suggest somewhere.' By which I mean I am not without powerful friends in this city.

'Maybe you better ask him quickly,' replies Casax, by which he means that I'm not fooling anyone.

Young Orius Fire Tamer is still standing in the street looking puzzled. His powers have brought him this far but wily old Astrath Triple Moon's improved spell of bafflement is preventing him from precisely locating

Quen. Casax returns to his side and speaks to him briefly. He's too important a man to spend his time hanging round in Quintessence Street, so after ordering his thugs to carry on the search he departs. Karlox scowls over at me, large, vicious and dumb as an Orc. There's nothing he'd like better than for Casax to order him to run me out of town. Let him try. I scowl back before shutting the door and rejoining Makri.

'We have to do something about Quen. The Brotherhood is close. Astrath's got their Sorcerer baffled but if the Guards bring Old Hasius the Brilliant in on the case we're sunk.'

'Are they still watching the place every night?'

I nod. 'But we might be able to sneak her away somehow. Maybe Astrath could work an invisibility spell for us. It's a lot to ask, though. Astrath has his own life to lead. We can't expect him to move heaven, earth and the three moons to help some young woman he's never met, especially as he risks getting into trouble with the Brotherhood.'

'If we do sneak her away,' enquires Makri, 'will she still be hidden by his bafflement spell?'

'No.'

'Then we can't do it.'

'What do you mean we can't do it?' I protest, getting angry. 'She can't stay here forever.'

'We can't just give her up to the Brotherhood.'

I suppose we can't. Not that I've grown attached to Quen or anything – she's a surly young woman as far as I can tell – but it would go against the grain to give up anyone or anything to Casax. I'm left with nothing much to say, so I just give Makri some abuse for landing me in this situation.

I notice that Palax has fallen asleep over his plate of food at the next table. It's a hard life being a busker. But I also notice Kaby is looking madder than a Troll with a toothache, which generally means only one thing. Palax did promise her he'd give up dwa, I seem to remember. It's a hard thing to give up. I grab a beer and take it upstairs with me where I lie on my couch and think about monks and statues and drift off to sleep.

I am awakened by a gentle knocking at my door.

'Who's there?' I call.

'Soolanis,' comes the reply.

I wondered where she'd disappeared to.

I go and open the door.

Soolanis is there. So is Sarin the Merciless, with a knife at her throat. Sarin shoves her inside and steps in after her.

'You could just have knocked.'

'I never like the thought of being turned away,' says Sarin, knife still in her hand.

Sarin the Merciless is a tall woman with her hair cut unusually short, rather austere in appearance apart from the many gold and silver rings in her ears. She wears a man's tunic. Her eyes are as black as Makri's but they lack that friendly twinkle. She stares at me, as if wondering whether to knife me on the spot. My hand is on my sword, just in case.

'I'm looking for a statue,' she says.

'That's a popular pastime round here these days.'

'Well? Where is it?'

'No idea. I presume you're talking about the statue that vanished when Drantaax was murdered? No one knows where it is.'

'I figure you do.'

'You figure wrong.'

'I know you've been hired to find it.'

'I'm puzzled, Sarin. What makes you think I'd discuss this with you?'

'I'll kill you if you don't.'

Sarin never has been one for working out unnecessarily subtle plans.

'You want it for the Star Temple?'

'That's right.'

I point out that Ixial the Seer will be dead soon.

'I think he'll live. And even if he doesn't, I'll help his followers.'

I ask her why. She confirms my suspicion – she studied fighting and meditation under Ixial, so she owes her loyalty to him. But I very much doubt if Sarin the Merciless feels loyal to anyone.

'Did you kill Drantaax?'

'I didn't come here to answer your questions. I came for the statue.'

'The statue weighed two tons. How could I have it?'

I study her face to see if she is aware of the magic purse, but Sarin is as cold as an Orc's heart and her face is impossible to read.

'Did you kill my father?' blurts out Soolanis.

'And who would that have been?'

'Thalius Green Eye.'

'No. And don't interrupt me again.'

Sarin turns to me. 'I want that statue, otherwise I'll kill you.'

'Well, thanks for the warning. I'm always happy to spend time with cheap killers. Which is what you are, skulking round corners with your crossbow. I'd run you in now if there was a reward on your head. Now get out.'

Sarin shows no signs of anger at my insults. She simply departs. I turn to Soolanis, who looks shaken by the affair.

'That may well be the woman who killed your father and she wouldn't think twice about killing you. Don't go to any more taverns on your own,' I warn her. 'Go home to Thamlin.'

'I don't want to go home,' she says miserably.

'Then get drunk downstairs.'

Needing no further encouragement she departs to do just that. I take the purse out of my pocket and stare at it. Inside this purse is a large statue which numerous people seem very keen to get hold of. Too keen, you might think. I mean, how fascinating can a statue be? I'm finding it increasingly hard to believe that the monasteries want it for their religious ceremonies. There must be easier ways of acquiring a statue, even at short notice. So why is everyone so eager to find it? It's only a lump of bronze. Bronze is moderately valuable, but not valuable enough to go around killing people for. By the time it was melted down and transported anywhere, it would hardly be worth the trouble.

All things considered, I'm starting to feel rather suspicious about this statue.

'You're going to what?'

'I'm going to smash the statue. Bring me a sledgehammer.'

Makri looks concerned. 'I know you're in a tough spot but there's no need to take it out on the statue. Couldn't you just talk things over with someone?'

'I'm not taking anything out on the statue. I want to see what's inside it.'

'Isn't it hollow?'

'Maybe. But I'm starting to have my doubts. Okay, it's a nice work of art. Okay, a monastery full of warrior monks needs a statue of Saint Quatinius or they can't show their faces at the monastery next door. And the Triple-Moon Conjunction is coming up soon. But why this statue? The True Church doesn't require anyone to observe their ceremonies in front of a particularly fine statue. Quite the opposite. They specifically say that worshippers can make do with virtually any old representation of the saint, which is why poor people everywhere observe the Triple-Moon Conjunction in front of cheap plaster artefacts. You can buy them in the market. You wouldn't expect that warrior monks, noted for their austerity, would absolutely have to have some fancy statue made by Turai's top sculptor. Doesn't make sense. As for Sarin the Merciless, she says she wants it for the Star Temple out of loyalty to Ixial. If you'll believe that you'll believe anything. That woman has about as much loyalty as a bokana snake.'

'I fought a bokana snake bare-handed in the arena one time.'

'Makri. Will you please stop this habit of reminiscing about the arena every time I mention some species of wildlife?'

'Sorry.'

The more I think about it, the more convinced I am that this is no ordinary statue. I'm determined to take a closer look. And by doing so I will yet again be breaking the law, because it is heresy to interfere in any way with a statue of Saint Quatinius and if the True Church knew I was about to assault one with a sledgehammer they'd have me up before the special Religious Court and off to a prison galley in less time than it takes Bishop Gzekius to guzzle down his evening decanter of fine Elvish wine.

'We can't let anyone see us or there'll be trouble. You make sure Soolanis, Quen and Dandelion are out of the way and I'll find a suitable heavy tool.'

Soolanis, Quen and Dandelion. Just saying the names makes me feel uncomfortable. How did I end up playing host to these three young women? And did they have to be a drunk, a whore and a freak of nature? Sometimes I don't know what the city is coming to.

'When I was young you'd have been locked up for walking round with flowers in your hair,' I grumble, heading downstairs to the courtyard at the back of the tavern.

There's a shed here, in which Palax and Kaby stable their horse. Behind this is their caravan. The sight makes me shudder. Normal people have plain wooden caravans painted white, with perhaps a little picture of Saint Quatinius in a yellow frame to bring them luck. Palax and Kaby's contraption is decorated with murals of God knows what in colours bright enough to sear the eyeball. With those young women upstairs and this pair of weirdos out here, I'm starting to feel annoyed. I marched through deserts and fought battles for these people. You think they might show some respect. Dress normally and get jobs, for instance.

I grab a weighty hammer from Gurd's tool collection and head back upstairs. I'm now thoroughly in a mood for smashing something. A large statue of the Blessed Saint Quatinius on horseback will do nicely.

Back in my room I carefully pull down the top of the purse. The head of the statue appears from out of the magic space. I have to be careful here, exposing enough of the statue for me to hit while keeping its base inside the magic space. If the statue were to appear fully in my room its weight might go right through the floor and kill half of the drinkers downstairs.

Makri is still dubious about the whole operation.

'It is a good statue,' she points out. 'Didn't you say it was an important work of art? Drantaax was a fine artist. I don't think it's right to destroy one of his works. Especially the last one he made before he was murdered.'

I brush her objections aside. Five months studying at the Guild College and she thinks she's an art expert.

'Stand well back.'

'You'll break your arm.'

I hadn't considered this. I'm not backing down now. I let go at Saint Quatinius's head, aiming at the hardly visible point under the chin where bronze panels have been soldered together. I give it a mighty blow, putting all my weight into it (and that's enough weight for anyone).

There is an almighty clang. A small dent appears. I hit it again. The dent gets bigger. I let go with another furious blow and this time the bronze panel falls right off, landing with a great clatter on the floor. And there, staring out at us like an angel from heaven, is a beautifully moulded golden face.

I practically yell in triumph. 'Gold! It's gold inside! That's what everybody's after.'

I'm happy as a drunken mercenary at getting this one right. 'This must be the missing gold, hijacked last month on the way from the mines to the King's treasuries. And I'm in a for a fat reward.'

I look at the golden head. Underneath it, still covered in bronze, will be a golden body. I doubt if there's ever been so much gold in Twelve Seas before. Worth so much I couldn't even calculate it. And no one knows I've got it.

Makri and I study it thoughtfully.

'Never see that much gold again,' I muse.

'Definitely not.'

'The King has an awful lot of gold already.'

'And they're digging more out of the ground all the time.'

I sigh, and start pulling the edges of the purse over the statue. It's a tempting thought but someone would find out eventually. I'm too old for the life of a fugitive.

'I guess I wouldn't want to leave Turai right now,' says Makri. 'The city stinks, but it has the best university in the west.'

The statue has now disappeared into the magic space. I put the purse back in my pocket.

'I suppose you could maybe just remove a finger before you give it back?'

'Absolutely not.'

Actually, that's not such a bad idea. I'll see how the money situation is. Of course, I'm due a big, big reward now. The King is as mad as a dragon over the loss of his gold and the Palace has offered a thousand gurans for information leading to its recovery. I could take the purse to the Imperial Palace right this minute and demand payment, except I'm still working to clear Grosex and find Thalius's killer, which means I still need the statue.

'Do you think the Star Temple and the Cloud Temple know that the gold is inside?'

'Yes.'

'Who put it there?'

'I'm not sure yet. Whoever it was, the monks want it badly. So does Sarin. So we can now expect all hell to break loose.'

That's fine with Makri. And it's fine with me right now, when I'm feeling pleased with myself for solving part of the mystery. I pick up a knife, toss it in the air so that it spins, catch it by the handle, and slip it into its scabbard in one easy movement. Then I get out my grimoire and start memorising the sleep spell.

'If they want it they're going to have to come and get it off me. I'll soon show them who's number one chariot in these parts.'

I take a bottle of klee from my table. It's empty. I seem to be going through it pretty quickly. I haul out another from my secret supply under the couch and share a couple of glasses with Makri. She shudders as it burns her throat.

'You're getting me into bad habits.'

'What bad habits? Incidentally, what's so great about fighting a bokana snake? I killed plenty of bokana snakes when we marched through the jungle. They're not *that* scary.'

'They grow much bigger in the Orc Lands. Deadlier poison as well.'

'Naturally.'

The sun's beating down and I'd be happy to spend the afternoon sleeping but I've work to do. As I strap on my sword and head on out, I remember I swore I wasn't going to work any more this summer. So much for that. If I pick up a nice reward for the stolen gold I'm going to spend the autumn and winter propping up Gurd's bar swapping war stories with anyone who cares to join me.

I notice two Brotherhood men in the area, still

nosing around, looking for Quen. And someone else I recognise as an Investigator from uptown, probably hired by the Innkeepers Guild. I scowl. All I need now is for Sarin to pop out from behind a wall and start firing crossbow bolts at me.

The main law courts are close to the business area of Golden Crescent. It's an important part of town and the law court itself is a splendid building with thirty columns at the front and a portico of gleaming white marble. It's situated in a large public forum with a fountain and statues of assorted saints and past kings. The whole thing was built for the glorification of the city a couple of hundred years ago by King Sarius-Akan after he defeated Mattesh in battle and arrived home with a fair amount of booty to spare.

I used to come here often when I was Senior Investigator at the Palace. Any time I walked in, attendants would greet me politely and barristers from the Abode of Justice would rush to meet me to see what news I brought of my investigations. Those days are long past. If anyone here recognises me, they don't show it. There's no point in being polite to a man who's lost all social status, and you can't lose much more social status than I did when I was bounced out of the Palace for drunken misbehaviour.

I finally get to see Grosex, in the underground cells. He's sitting on a small wooden bunk and looks as if he hasn't slept or eaten for some time.

'How did the first day of the trial go?'

'Badly.'

'How's your public defender?'

'Still reading up on the case.'

Grosex is pale and noticeably thinner than he was a week ago when they arrested him. I can tell he's a man who's given up hope. I try and reassure him, telling him I'm following up a number of leads and so on.

'I expect to have the real killer soon.'

'Soon enough to stop them from hanging me?'

'Of course.'

That's close to a lie. The trial probably won't last more than another two days. If he's convicted he'll be executed soon after that. Turai's judiciary waste no time once they've found someone guilty. As a full citizen of Turai, Grosex will have the right of appeal to the King if sentenced to death, but the King never likes to buck public opinion by being too lenient. He's worried it'll give Senator Lodius's Populares a stick to beat him with, with crime being so bad in the city these days.

I question Grosex intensely for an hour and I don't learn anything. As far as he was concerned, it was just another day at the workshop till he found Drantaax with a knife sticking in him.

'When did you last use the knife?'

He doesn't remember exactly, but he used it at work frequently so it was bound to have his aura on it. I tell him not to worry.

'There's plenty of ways to fake a man's aura on a knife. I'll get to the bottom of it.'

I wonder out loud if Calia might have killed her husband, but Grosex doesn't think this is likely. He knows she was bored, but she didn't hate him. On the contrary, she was rather grateful that she didn't have to live in Twelve Seas any more.

'You know anything about some illegal gold?'

He looks at me blankly. I don't tell him the full facts about the golden statue, but I let him know that Drantaax was mixed up in the gold heist somehow.

Grosex vehemently denies that the sculptor could have had any part in the crime. I'm certain that Drantaax couldn't possibly have filled up the bronze statue with gold in his workshop without his apprentice being aware of it so I tell him not to bother putting on an act.

'Drantaax is dead, so you don't have to defend him. And you haven't much time left. Figuring out where Drantaax acquired the gold might get me to his killer more quickly, so if you know anything you better spill it right now.'

Poor, thin, pale Grosex seems to give up completely. He slumps on the hard wooden chair, his head in his hands, staring at the bare stone floor.

'I knew he would never get away with it,' he sighs. 'Now he's dead. If you expose him he won't even have his reputation left.'

'You like his reputation more than your own life?'

Grosex considers it. Finally he decides that he likes his life better but it's a closely run thing. He doesn't feel like struggling any more. I think he might even be starting to regard the noose as a welcome release. I never like it when my clients get like that.

'It was the gambling that started it.'

'Gambling?'

'Drantaax would bet on anything. He was never

away from the Stadium Superbius in the chariot season. Other times he'd place bets on the out-of-town tracks. It got so he was in so much debt everywhere we could hardly get a delivery of marble any more.'

I start to warm to Drantaax. He doesn't sound like such a bad guy for an artist.

'Did he drink?'

'Way too much.'

You think these artists are dull and they turn out to be okay after all.

'He'd remortgaged the house, and he was about to lose it. Calia knew nothing about it and he was desperate she shouldn't find out.' He laughs ruefully. 'Not that she would have cared particularly. Poor Drantaax was crazy about her, but she didn't care anything for him. I figure she was involved with someone else, but I don't know who. People thought it was me, but they were wrong.'

So Drantaax, heavily in debt, addled by drink and desperate for a way out of trouble, was more than interested when a solution presented itself in the form of a visitor who made the unusual enquiry as to whether the sculptor could hide a large amount of gold inside a statue. The new statue of Saint Quatinius to be precise.

'Why Saint Quatinius?'

'Because it's heretical to interfere with a statue of the saint. Even if Sorcerers from the Abode of Justice were scanning the city looking for the gold, they would never look inside a statue of Quatinius. It would be blasphemous.'

That's true. It hadn't occurred to me before. Sorcerers have a shaky relationship with the True Church at the best of times. No Sorcerer is going to risk the wrath of the Church by interfering with its most important religious icon.

'The plan was to let the gold stay in the statue when it was placed outside the city in the shrine, then remove it later when the heat died down. Drantaax was paid enough to cover his debts and get his business back on its feet.'

'Who was behind it?'

Grosex doesn't know. He never even saw the person who made the arrangements. Drantaax told him about it as it was impossible to hide the operation, but Grosex is very hazy on the details. He has no idea who might have killed Drantaax. He doesn't seem to know much about anything, and I can't prise any knowledge of the monks or Sarin from him.

'Who else knew about the gold heist?'

'No one. Drantaax swore me to secrecy. I never breathed a word.'

'Didn't it bother you to get caught up in this? Even if Drantaax hadn't been murdered, you were quite likely to end up in jail as an accessory to stealing the King's gold.'

'What could I do? Go and report my employer to the authorities? No other sculptor would ever take me on to finish my apprenticeship. I'd have been in trouble with the authorities anyway. No one would have believed I wasn't involved. Besides, Drantaax was the greatest artist in the city. One of the greatest any-

where. I didn't want to be the man responsible for
sending him to a prison ship.'

A Guard enters the cell to tell me that time is up. I
discreetly slip Grosex a couple of thazis sticks before I
depart. Might cheer him up a little. I care for my
clients. It's illegal, of course, but what can they do to a
guy they're going to hang soon anyway?

'I'll have you free in no time,' I say in parting, as
much to impress the Guard as anything. A brief
depression settles on me. Ever since I saw the miserable little room in Twelve Seas where Grosex lived, and
learned that he had no friends or family, I've been trying to avoid feeling sorry for him. Seeing him sit there
in his cell waiting to be hanged, it's impossible not to.

'Well, you look as miserable as a Niojan whore,'
comes a robust voice.

It's Captain Rallee. I scowl at him, and stop looking
miserable. I'm not going to let Captain Rallee know
that I've started to pity my clients. He tells me I'm just
the man he's looking for.

'Still trying to clear Grosex? Leaving it a bit late,
aren't you?'

'I'd have been further on if Prefect Tholius hadn't
arranged things so I couldn't see my client.'

The Captain shrugs. 'Tholius never bothers with
the fine points of the law. He's a fool. Dumb as an Orc
in fact. But it makes little difference in this case because
Grosex is guilty, as you probably know by now.'

'No evidence he did it.'

'No evidence? It was his knife, and his aura was all
over it.'

'Come on, Rallee. There's plenty of ways to fake that.'

'No. There are only a few ways to fake it. And they all need grade-A skills in sorcery. Are you saying that some high-level Sorcerer went all the way to Drantaax's workshop just so he could stick a knife in the sculptor and blame the apprentice? Not too likely. Anyway, it didn't happen, because Old Hasius the Brilliant says no sorcery was used in the workshop and I'll take his word above yours any day. So will the court.'

'What motive could he have?'

'Calia probably. Kill the employer and set up with his wife. It's not smart, but it's not uncommon either. I remember you covered a couple of cases like that before you got slung out the Palace. Face it, Thraxas, you're on a loser with this one. When it comes down to pulling dumb strokes like trying to get me to believe that two thugs off the street who attacked you also killed Drantaax, it's time to hand in your toga. But that's not what I wanted to see you about. What's going on with the monks that are infesting the city?'

'Monks infesting the city? I hadn't noticed.'

'Sure you haven't, Thraxas. Except you have one for a client. The Venerable Tresius. Better make sure you don't annoy him, he was empty-hand-fighting champion of the Northern Army forty years back. I hear he hasn't withered with age. What's he hired you for?'

Captain Rallee should know by now that I never discuss my clients' affairs with the Civil Guard.

'He didn't hire me. He just dropped in to swap a few ideas about consubstantiality. '

'And what the hell is that?'

'A complicated religious matter relating to the precise nature of the Divinity.'

'Funny, Thraxas, funny. Is that what you were discussing when you were hauling your fat butt over the wall up at the villa in Thamlin the other night? Don't look so surprised. You're not so hard to identify. Neither is Makri. The Guards who saw you going over the wall tell me you still move well for such a big man. What was the fighting about?'

'Sorry, Captain. I really don't know what it was about. Myself and Makri were just out on some private business and we happened upon it.'

'No good, Thraxas. Whatever the monks are up to, you're involved in it. Taking a lot of work on, aren't you? The Venerable Tresius, Thalius's daughter . . . and Quen.'

I almost jump when the captain says this, but I control myself. I'm appalled that the Captain knows about Quen. Maybe I should've expected it – he's a good man with any number of contacts – but the news that I am being linked to Quen comes as a blow.

'If you're hiding her, Thraxas, you're in for a whole lot of trouble. She burned down that tavern and killed the landlord and she's due a short trip to the gallows. She won't even make it as far as the gallows if the Brotherhood find her first. And neither will you. What did you get involved for?'

I can't think of a snappy answer so I remain silent.

'If you know where she is, Thraxas, and you're holding out, I really advise you to think again. Tell me and I'll take her away quietly so that no one connects it with you.'

Distant memories of us fighting the Niojans and the Orcs together must be stirring inside Rallee. He's trying to do me a favour here. Prevent me from falling foul of the Brotherhood. While I'd certainly like Quen off my hands, I'm not turning a friend of Makri's over to the authorities for them to string her up. I stay silent, and make to leave.

'I think you're being unwise on this one, Thraxas. You have too much on your plate already. These monks are tearing each other to pieces. Whatever your involvement, you'll probably end up getting torn apart yourself. Especially now Ixial's back on his feet. A dangerous man, Ixial the Seer.'

I gape in astonishment. 'Ixial the Seer? Back on his feet? He was next best thing to dead a couple of hours ago.'

'Maybe. But he's walking around just fine now. I've seen him. We had him in for questioning about the fight in the garden. And I know one other thing I'll tell you for free. There's an Assassin's contract out on him.'

'How do you know that?'

'We have our sources.'

'If you've got a spy in the Assassins Guild it's liable to be a very short stay. Have they really been hired to assassinate Ixial?'

'Yes. I'd stay well out of it if I was you, Thraxas. If you can find who killed old Thalius Green Eye, good luck to you. I'd even wish you good luck if you could come up with anything to clear Grosex, even though he's guilty as hell. But you ought to steer clear of those monks. And ditch Quen before the Brotherhood starts getting annoyed or the Abode of Justice assigns a proper Sorcerer to hunt for her.'

I walk out of the law courts with much on my mind. Ixial is alive. He can't be, but he is. And now there's a contract out on him. From who? And for why? Damn these monks. I wish I'd never met any of them. And damn that Quen as well. If she had to go and burn down a tavern, couldn't she have just climbed on a horse and ridden out of town, instead of coming to the Avenging Axe and making my life difficult?

I meant to ask the Captain if the Guard was making any progress on the missing gold. I forgot. It's hot. I find a tavern next door and push my way through the scribes and jurists and petitioners of the law courts to get one beer to quench my thirst and another to encourage some serious thinking.

CHAPTER
THIRTEEN

Makri flops down on my couch. Perspiration runs down her shoulders and she rubs her skin where the chainmail bikini has been chafing in the heat.

'Stupid garment,' she mutters.

It certainly is. No protection at all in a fight. Makri has an excellent set of lightweight leather and chainmail body armour which she brought with her from the gladiator pits. Orcs are skilful metalsmiths and their armour is easily a match for ours, if not quite up to the standard of the Elves. Makri's light mail will turn most blades, but it doesn't turn heads – or earn tips, hence the bikini during working hours. All fairly undignified, I suppose, but as Makri regards all men in Twelve Seas as scum she doesn't really care. She is, however, starting to care about the congestion in her room.

'Throw Dandelion out,' I suggest, hopefully.

'No. I said she could stay.'

'Doesn't she live anywhere?'

'She doesn't seem to. She's been sleeping on the beach recently.'

'Well, at least she's close to the dolphins.'

Makri won't go back on her word, so Dandelion

stays for the meantime, but she does admit that it's starting to be a strain. Dandelion keeps wanting to do her horoscope and Makri doesn't really have the time for this sort of thing. Also she lit some perfumed candles which dripped wax all over Makri's axe. Which was annoying for a woman who loves her axe.

'Why do you put up with it?'

'I like her, sort of. I never met anyone before who thought trees were as important as people. Anyway, I don't have any friends in this city. Except for you, I suppose. It's good to have someone else to talk to. At least she's friendlier than Quen – Quen never speaks. You'd think she might be more civil, seeing that I'm saving her life by letting her live here.'

I suggest that Quen might have been too soured by her experiences as an exotic dancer to be friendly to anyone any more. Or maybe she's too scared of the Brotherhood to think about small talk.

'Maybe. But all she does is sit there in silence. It's a bit of a strain. How come I've ended up with Soolanis as well?'

'I think she's too unhappy about her father being killed to go back home. I expect it gets lonely in a villa on your own.'

'Couldn't she sleep in here?'

'Absolutely not. I need the couch for whenever I can't make it into the bedroom. You're too soft, Makri. If you don't want her around, just throw her out. No one's trying to kill her.'

Makri grunts. 'Well she's not much trouble. Just lies around drunk all day.'

It's interesting the way she's gathered a group of troubled young women around her. She could start holding her own branch meetings of the Association of Gentlewomen. Provided they allowed for wide interpretation of the word 'Gentlewomen'. They let Makri in, so I guess they must.

Makri has come along to study her notes for her next class, as it's too crowded in her own room to concentrate.

'What are you studying?'

'Elvish languages.'

'You speak Elvish already.'

'Only the common tongue. I'm learning the royal language.'

I'm not sure how come Makri speaks Elvish. She's quarter Elvish of course, but I assume the Elvish grandparent wasn't around in the gladiator pits. She never volunteers information about her upbringing, and I've never asked.

'What's that?' she enquires, noticing that I have a sheet of paper in front of me on the desk.

'I've been making a list of everything I need to deal with. It's something I do when I get too many things going on to remember at once.'

I pass it over and she reads it out.

'Monks, statue, gold robbery, Drantaax, Grosex, Thalius, Assassins Guild, Quen, Sarin, Ixial, Tresius. You're right. You do have too many things to remember. Funny how you weren't going to do any work this summer.'

'Hilarious.'

'You can cross Ixial off now anyway.'

'No, I can't. He's walking around healthy.'

'Don't be ridiculous.'

I assure her it's true. Makri is just as astonished as me. She knows as well as I do that Ixial should be dead by now. Even if he somehow managed to cheat death, he'd be recuperating for months. There is just no way he could be up and about.

'Sorcery?'

'No sorcery I've ever heard of can cure gangrene and heal wounds like that. I just don't know.'

'What's the Assassins Guild doing on the list?'

'They've been engaged to kill Ixial. Don't know who by, but it's reliable information. He's not going to be an easy target from what I hear. If your friend Hanama gets the job, she'd better watch out.'

Makri stiffens slightly at the mention of Hanama, wondering if we're going to have our standard disagreement about the subject, but the moment passes without dispute.

'And take care when you're out. Sarin the Merciless is threatening to shoot on sight if I don't hand over the statue.'

'I will. Are you close to digging up anything to clear Grosex?'

'Not really. I strongly suspect those two guys we fought here but now they're gone up in smoke there's no way of connecting them with the crime. Even if they did carry out the killing, I figure someone else organised it. If I could prove that I'd still get the apprentice off. Everything revolves round the statue, which does point towards Ixial and the Star Temple, but now it's turned out to be full of gold who's to say it wasn't someone else altogether? Maybe whoever organised the heist fell out with Drantaax and had him killed. It could just be a coincidence that right at that moment the Star Temple came looking for a statue. Or else Ixial knew about the gold and was in on it all along. I just don't know. I can't turn up in court with some wild story about monks and statues. If the Consul found out I had the gold he'd be more likely to hang me than clear Grosex.'

I take a drink of beer and a mouthful from a pastry I got at Minarixa's fine bakery. 'What I need is some inspiration. Or a stroke of luck. Either will do.'

'How long till they hang Grosex?'

'Two or three days.'

'Well, at least there's no hurry. Have another beer.'

I note that Makri's sarcasm is coming along nicely. She settles down with her Elvish manuscript and I stare vacantly out of the window, waiting for inspiration. I've got too much information. I can't sort it out. I'm confused. I go downstairs and bring up another beer.

Some hours later I'm still staring out of the window, though now I have a pile of empty flagons at my feet. Makri, who has been busy reading all this time, finally rises from the floor and folds up her manuscript. She casts a glance at the empty flagons.

'It's been a pleasure to watch you at work,' she says, grinning. She heads downstairs to the back yard for a little weapons practice before her Elvish languages class.

I sigh. Inspiration never arrived. And I gave it every opportunity. I suppose I'd better just go out and see if I can stir things up a little. I'll go and visit Ixial the Seer. Even if I don't learn anything new about the case, he might let me into his health secrets.

I load up with a vast tray of stew and assorted vegetables from Tanrose. Just audible from outside are the sounds of a young woman attacking a target dummy with an axe and assorted swords and knives.

'Makri tells me she's making good progress at the Guild College,' says Tanrose.

'Yes. She'll be talking to the Elvish Royal Family in their own language soon. I wonder if they'll talk back to her?'

Tanrose's stew fails to provide me with the pleasure it normally does. I take an extra pancake to mop up my plate, but my heart isn't really in it. In a morose mood I head out into the afternoon heat to see what I can dig up.

'Better than rowing a slave galley I suppose,' I mutter to myself, striding up Quintessence Street.

A bunch of young Koolu Kings are hanging around at the first corner, trying to look tough. They stare at me as I go past. I stare back. They'll all be in the Brotherhood soon enough, ready for the real world of crime, unless war breaks out and they get conscripted, in which case most of them will be dead. Or the plague strikes like it did a few years back – another good way of emptying the slums.

I find a landus quickly and direct the driver to the villa in Thamlin. I'm in two minds as to whether to make a direct approach to Ixial or whether to try sneaking quietly in the back. I decide on the direct approach. I've had enough of sneaking for now.

My direct approach achieves results. After marching up to the villa and banging on the front door loudly enough to wake Old King Kiben it's answered by Calia herself. It's odd the way there don't seem to be any servants here. I suppose the monks must look after themselves. At any other abode in Thamlin the women of the house would rather die than actually answer the door themselves, but I suppose that Calia, coming from Twelve Seas, doesn't mind so much.

Calia informs me no one is in. She stands in the door in a manner to suggest I'm not welcome to come in and check. I notice she's looking happier with life.

'I hear Ixial got well.'

She nods.

'How?'

'Through his great powers of recovery.'

'Amazing powers. Almost makes me want to take up meditation. Where is he? Looking for Tresius?'

If she knows she isn't saying.

I tell her I'd like to ask a few questions about Drantaax. She doesn't want to talk till I point out that she's still wanted by the Guards for questioning and I'm not above turning her in. This gets me inside the door, but not much further. According to Calia she knows no more than she told me before. She doesn't know who killed her husband, and she doesn't seem to know anything about illegal gold.

'You know Drantaax was heavily in debt?'

'No he wasn't. He was the most successful sculptor in the city. He had commissions for years to come, all of them worth money.'

'Maybe, but he liked to gamble. The way I hear it he'd remortgaged the house to pay off the book-makers, and he was about to lose everything.'

For the first time Calia looks surprised, then angry. She insists I must be mistaken.

'Drantaax didn't gamble. He might not have been so dull if he did. And he didn't drink. I don't know who you've been talking to, but none of it's true.'

So Drantaax managed to conceal his debts from his wife. And his drinking. Lucky man.

'If he wasn't in debt, why was he so worried about finishing this statue?'

'He wasn't worried,' claims Calia. 'It was on schedule. We took a few days off in the country right before he was killed. That's how worried he was. Now, excuse me, I have things to do.'

'Like what?'

'Packing. I'm leaving with Ixial.'

'You're leaving Grosex to hang.'

'There's nothing I can do about that. Nothing I can tell the Guards would clear his name.'

'Ixial being arrested for murder would clear his name.'

She falls silent. I can't get anything more out of her. Quite possibly she has nothing more to tell. Before I go I warn her about the Assassins. Ixial's welfare doesn't concern me but I hate the Assassins Guild for being a bunch of cold-hearted killers, and I'll frustrate them if

I can. Besides, if they kill Ixial I'm never going to bring him to court.

'Ixial the Seer can look out for himself.'

'I'm sure he can. But pass on the information anyway. The Assassins Guild is no joke. If Hanama takes the case, I don't reckon much for his chances. She won't bother marching up for a fair fight like the Venerable Tresius. She'll put an arrow in his back or use a poison dart while he's sleeping.'

As I'm leaving the villa I have the slight impression that there's something close by that doesn't belong. Something or someone. I can't quite make out what. The sensitivity that I developed during my Sorcerer's training rarely lets me down even now. It wouldn't surprise me if there was an Assassin in the garden. Well, I warned Ixial. If he ignores me, that's his problem.

I figure I should check on the gambling debts. I call in on Starox, the bookie, who operates from an illegal shop between Pashish and Twelve Seas. Starox is a Brotherhood man but we're on good terms, largely because I've lost so much money to him. To my surprise Starox tells me that he never took a bet from Drantaax.

I can't work out why not. If the sculptor wanted to gamble then Starox is the obvious person for him to transact his business with. What's more, Starox is of the opinion that if Drantaax was making large losses with any other bookmaker in town he'd have been bound to know about it.

'I know every heavy gambler in Turai. I don't figure

the sculptor as a gambler, Thraxas. He was a well-known man and as far as I know he never made a bet.'

I thank Starox. I also place a couple of bets before I leave. It's not the racing season in Turai – it's too hot for the chariots to run at the Stadium Superbius – but there's a small amphitheatre and track further down the coast where they catch the breeze off the sea and they're holding a race meeting this week. I was planning to go before I got bound up in this affair.

My next stop is the Public Records Office, which isn't far from the law courts. It's another place I used to be welcome but where the officials now pretend not to know me. To hell with them. I find a young clerk with time on his hands and we hunt through the scrolls in the records room till we find a document relating to Drantaax's property in Pashish.

'Who owns it?'

'Drantaax.'

'But who's holding the mortgage?'

'No one. According to the city records it isn't mortgaged.'

I take a look myself. He's right. Drantaax owned it outright. No problems with his finances are recorded here.

No debts and no gambling? Then why did Grosex think he was in such trouble? Stranger and stranger. I walk home, stopping off at a market stall to buy a watermelon which I eat, very messily, as I walk along.

It strikes me that if Sarin the Merciless carries out her threat then a bolt from her crossbow would go through me about as easily as the watermelon.

There's not much I can do about that except be careful
and rely on my senses to give me some sort of warning. I can't walk around wearing a breastplate in this
heat. It'd kill me just about as quick as the crossbow. I
could place the personal protection spell in my mind I
suppose, but that's a large spell and I find it tiring to
carry it around these days. Also, I like to have the sleep
spell handy when I'm on a case, and I can't carry
both. I just don't have the capacity any more.

I finally manage to track down one of Drantaax's
servants, a groom. The Guard had been holding him
as a material witness but his father has some influence
with the Horse Masters Guild and managed to spring
him. He doesn't tell me much I don't already know,
but he does confirm Calia's story that Drantaax
seemed to be in no trouble. The statue was coming
along on schedule and he doesn't know of any debts.
The groom had accompanied Drantaax and Calia on
their short break to Ferias, a small town further down
the coast where it's a little cooler in the summer.
People with money to spare often take a break there at
this time of year. Lucky them, I reflect, as the sweat
pours down inside my tunic and my leather sandals
start to feel as if they're made of wet rags.

I wonder if Drantaax had a bank account? Most of
the population never have enough money to worry
about banking it, and small businessmen usually just
keep their own safe or hide their takings somewhere in
their property but a relatively well-off man like Drantaax might possibly have kept an account up in Golden
Crescent where the upper classes transact their

business. I have few contacts in that area but I might be able to nose something out. It would answer the question of whether or not Drantaax was in debt. I'm preoccupied with these sort of thoughts so I don't notice Makri till she stumbles into me in Quintessence Street.

'Hey, watch your feet, Makri. What's the matter, the heat getting to you?'

'Sorry.'

She tells me she's just back from her class in advanced Elvish languages, which she finds stressful because the Professor always stares at her as if she shouldn't be there.

'I hate him. But listen.'

She says something in the Royal Elvish language.

'What did that mean?'

'Welcome to my tree.'

'Very good, Makri.'

'Are you impressed?'

'Yes. So will the Elves be if you ever sail down south and start talking it to them. Very few Humans learn the royal language.'

Not many Humans know any Elvish at all, though the Elves have no objections to people learning. Makri's Common Elvish is quite fluent already, and mine isn't too bad. You study some when you start off as a Sorcerer's Apprentice, and I had a chance to practise it when I visited the Elves.

One thing that Makri actually admires me for is that I've been to the Southern Islands. Few men have. We trade with them of course, but apart from the ships' crews, few citizens would ever venture that far, deeming it much too dangerous a voyage. It might not be worth the trouble anyway. We like the Elves here, but they don't welcome too many visitors.

'I will sail down there one day,' says Makri.

I'm surprised.

'What's brought that on? The last Elf you saw went as white as a sheet when he sensed your Orc blood. You swore you'd never even try speaking to one again.'

'Well, they'll be pleased to see me one day.'

Perhaps they will. For a social outcast Makri does have a surprising capacity for winning people over. And legendary creatures. When we visited the Fairy Glade a few months ago the Centaurs couldn't get enough of her. Of course Centaurs are, frankly, interested in any woman as well developed as Makri, no matter what her breeding.

'Kaby has a ring through her navel,' says Makri. 'I like it. Do you think I should get one?'

I'm bewildered by this sudden change of subject.

'You told me body piercing was taboo for the Elves,' Makri explains. 'Were you making it up?'

'No, it's true.'

'Well, I suppose I could always take it out when the time comes. Do you think I should get my nipples done?'

'Only if you want to completely panic the Elves. And what the hell would you want to do it for? No one's ever going to see.'

Makri has never had a lover. She says she might be

interested if all the men in Twelve Seas weren't so disgusting. I admit she has a point.

'Kaby has her nipples pierced. She was showing me—'

'Could we please change the subject? Guild classes are fine. Intimate bodily detail I can live without.'

Makri claims to be puzzled. 'Is this another of your "civilisation" things?'

Suddenly the call for Sabav, evening prayers, rings out.

'Now see what you've done, Makri. If you hadn't started rambling on about body piercing we'd have made it home before prayers. I could be sitting on my couch with a beer. Now we have to kneel down here and pray.'

There is no getting around this. Wherever you are when the call comes from the tall towers, you pray.

Most people, more aware of this obligation than myself and Makri, have departed either to their homes or a temple, either to pray or to hide until it's over, but there are a few other stragglers and, along with the people who live on the streets and don't have anywhere else to go, we kneel down. It's annoying, especially as the Avenging Axe is now in sight, but there's nothing to be done about it. Makri is particularly unwilling to carry out this act of devotion as she doesn't believe in the True Church, but no exceptions are allowed and failure to comply means arrest.

I mumble my way through the evening prayers. The sun is still beating down and the ground is hard on my knees. I console myself with the thought of Gurd's ale only a few minutes away. After what seems like a long time the call comes for the end of prayers. At that very instant I get a strong feeling that something is wrong. Some danger is very close. I'm halfway to my feet but I fling myself to the ground. There's the whizzing sound of a crossbow bolt and I feel a sharp pain in my arm as something nicks it. On my way to the ground I crash into Makri and we fall in a heap. I look up. There's blood on my arm, but I'm otherwise okay.

'Damn that Sarin,' I say, drawing my sword.

I notice that Makri isn't moving. She's lying face down in the dirt. I roll her over gently. There's a crossbow bolt sticking in her chest. Sarin's bolts are nine inches long. This one has penetrated about eight inches into Makri. Blood pours from the wound. I put my hand to her throat. I can't feel a pulse. I put my face next to her mouth; she isn't breathing. The lethal bolt aimed at me has smashed its way through her breastbone. Makri is dead.

CHAPTER FOURTEEN

For the first time in my life I'm frozen with horror. I don't look up to see if Sarin is in sight. I don't even try to get out of the way of another bolt. I just stare at Makri lying dead on the street in front of me.

Some people who were praying close by edge towards us. I take no notice of them as I pick up Makri's body and start walking helplessly back to the Avenging Axe.

'Call the Guards,' shouts someone.

It's too late for the Guards to do any good. I can't believe that this has happened. Makri's body is light in my arms and hangs limply as I take the last few steps to the tavern. Blood seeps from her chest over my arms. In the early evening the tavern is quiet. I walk to the bar, where Gurd, polishing tankards, looks up at me. His mouth falls open. I stand there stupidly, not knowing what to do next. I can hardly even speak.

Tanrose appears.

'Makri's dead,' I say eventually.

Tanrose takes my arm and leads me through to the room at the back and I lay the body on a table.

Gurd is as much in shock as myself and also cannot speak. Tanrose asks what happened.

'Sarin shot her,' I say.

Now I'm going to kill Sarin. But I can't bear to leave Makri's body.

Tanrose bends over her. Her eyes fill with tears. As the initial shock wears off my eyes start to brim over too. I feel sick. Gurd groans and sits down in despair.

I look at the body.

'She can't just be dead,' I say.

Makri suddenly coughs and blood spurts from her mouth. She groans faintly, then her body goes limp again.

'She's still alive!' cries Tanrose.

I waste no time talking. The second Makri coughs I'm off through the tavern on my way to Chiaraxi, the healer. Chiaraxi lives not far away. She's a skilful woman, ministering to the needs of the Twelve Seas poor for little reward but a great deal of gratitude. I run like I haven't run since I was a young man in the Army. At the entrance to Chiaraxi's tenement I find a queue of people waiting to go in. I barge my way past them into the apartment. There's a young woman there taking appointments in a waiting room. She looks up and starts to speak but I'm past and into the healer's room before she has a word out.

Chiaraxi is bending over a patient.

'Makri's got a crossbow bolt in her chest. She'll die any minute.'

I'm half expecting an argument and am quite prepared to pick up Chiaraxi and carry her to the Avenging Axe. To her credit, however, she nods, mutters something to her patient about seeing him tomorrow, and grabs her bag before hurrying out into the street at my side. We run back to the Avenging Axe, and I rush her through to the back room.

Makri shows no sign of life. Her skin has taken on a peculiar hue.

When Chiaraxi sees the crossbow bolt buried deep in her chest she glances questioningly at me.

'She's still alive,' I state. 'Do what you can. I'll get Astrath Triple Moon.'

I hurry out the back and saddle up Gurd's old horse as quickly as any old soldier in the country would. Then I leap on, ram my feet into the stirrups and ride furiously up Quintessence Street, careless of the pedestrians who scream abuse at me as I bowl them over. I make it from Twelve Seas to Pashish in record time and I don't waste any words on Astrath's servant as I shove him out the way at the front door and charge into Astrath's private room.

Less than a minute later we're heading back to the Avenging Axe. Astrath doesn't specialise in healing like some Sorcerers, but he has much knowledge and power. I'm praying he'll be able to help.

The horse protests as I mercilessly urge it on. It's on its last legs when it deposits myself and the Sorcerer at the tavern. I hurry Astrath through to where Makri lies motionless with Chiaraxi standing over her. She's stopped the bleeding.

'Is she alive?' I demand.

'Just.'

'She shouldn't be,' mutters Astrath, as he studies the wound, and Chiaraxi agrees with him. Astrath takes out a small clear crystal. It's a lifestone, carried by most Sorcerers. One of its properties is that when held next to a person's skin it glows with a green light. Unless they're dead. Then it doesn't glow at all. Astrath presses it on Makri's forehead. We strain to make out any colouring in the crystal. At first nothing happens and then, with painful slowness, the tiniest flicker of green appears.

Astrath stands up, looking troubled. He doesn't seem to want to say anything. I tell him to spit it out.

'No one recovers from that,' he says, glancing at the crystal, which has already returned to its colourless state.

It seems clear that only Makri's great inner strength, derived from her mixed blood, has kept her alive. Even that is fading now.

'Take the bolt out!' screams Gurd suddenly, as his emotions pour out in a great burst.

Chiaraxi shakes her head. The bolt is buried in the bone. Even attempting to move it will kill Makri for sure.

'I've given her amacia herb,' she says. 'It'll strengthen her. I can't do any more.'

Astrath speaks a spell over the body. I recognise it as a spell for strengthening the body's resistance. Very good if you have the plague. Not so helpful if you have eight inches of crossbow bolt buried inside you. Astrath and Chiaraxi hold out no hope. The amacia herb and the spell will do no more than delay the inevitable, and not for long. They can't even estimate how long Makri will stay alive, as she should be dead already. So I can't think of anything to do but wait till she dies then go and kill Sarin.

'What's happening?'

It's Dandelion. She yells in horror when she sees Makri. I'm too upset by events to care. My sleeves are still wet with Makri's blood.

Dandelion turns to me. 'The dolphins' healing stone!'

So desperate is the situation that I'm prepared to grasp at the straw. 'The healing stone? Is it real?'

'Of course it's real. I keep telling you. It will heal anything, but it was stolen.'

A flash of inspiration strikes. One that should have struck before. Ixial the Seer. He couldn't recover from his wounds, but he did.

'What's the healing stone like?' I demand.

'I don't know.'

'What do you mean, you don't know?' I roar.

Dandelion quails, thinking I'm about to strike her. I might.

'I never asked them what it was like. I just know it's their healing stone.'

I want to rush off and find Ixial but I force myself to calm down and think. No use running blindly around town not even knowing what I'm looking for. The dolphins that talk live out in the bay. It's about a twenty-minute ride there. Too long.

'I could try calling from the harbour,' says Dandelion. 'They sometimes swim close enough to hear.'

I agree to try. And I ask Astrath if he can locate Ixial for me.

'Maybe, if you have something belonging to him. Otherwise, maybe not.'

I don't have anything. Or anything he's touched. I rack my brains for inspiration. There's the gold in the statue. If he was behind the bullion robbery he might have touched that.

I take out the magic purse and drag the top of it down. In the general horror about what has happened to Makri no one even gasps as the statue appears.

Astrath Triple Moon shakes his head. 'No use, Thraxas. It's been in the magic space. Any lingering aura will be wiped off.'

I step outside and return with the sledgehammer, then smash more of the bronze covering off, revealing a fresh piece of gold. 'How about that? It's been covered all the time it's been in there.'

Astrath fingers his short grey beard. 'I might get something.'

'Do what you can, then meet me at the bottom of Moon and Stars Avenue.'

Gurd's old horse won't make another journey with two people on its back. I hurry along Quintessence Street with Dandelion, looking for a landus. The first one that trots past has some sort of minor official in the back. I grab the reins, bringing it to a halt, then brandish my sword.

'Need this landus,' I say.

He leaps out, uttering threats. I punch him, and he falls down.

'Take us to the harbour and make it quick,' I tell the driver.

I'm still carrying my sword. He takes us to the harbour, and he makes it quick.

Dandelion says she once talked to a dolphin at the furthest edge of the longest pier. We head there, out past the triremes and biremes docked for loading and unloading. The hulks are quiet in the evening, each burning only a small harbour light at the bow and stern. A few Securitus men, hired by the harbour authority, patrol the docks at night, but we encounter no one as we run along the pier. I don't run too far these days, as a rule. I feel my heart pounding with the effort, but I ignore it. Dandelion stumbles and falls. I drag her up. She's cut her foot on a sharp piece of metal and leaves a blood-stained footprint behind as we rush on. At the furthest part of the harbour is a breakwater which juts far out into the sea, providing shelter from the wind for incoming vessels. We stop when we can go no further.

'Well?' I demand.

Dandelion looks out over the dark sea. The sun has dipped over the horizon, its last rays casting a dark red hue over the water. Like wine, as I believe an Elvish poet once said. Dandelion tilts her head slightly and emits a very strange sound, a high-pitched whine with clicks and gurgles mixed in. We wait. Nothing happens. She does it again. I glance at her with fury. If this is her idea of a joke I'm going to throw her into the sea.

'Where are the dolphins?' I practically scream.

She makes the noise a third time. I'm about to turn on my heels and go off looking for Ixial when she suddenly calls and points. Right underneath us a dolphin has poked its head through the surface and looks at Dandelion expectantly.

'What'll I say?'

'Tell it I'm here to find the healing stone. And tell it I have no time to waste.'

They gurgle and whistle to each other for what seems like an eternity, though I suppose it's reasonably fast for a conversation between a dolphin and a human. Dandelion finally turns to me and tells me that the dolphins' healing stone is vaguely cross-shaped, made of black stone and about the size of a man's hand. That seems like enough to be going on with.

'It was on the altar of their undersea temple far off in the bay and a diver took it when they were all playing out at sea. The temple is—'

'Tell me the details later,' I grunt. I head off, leaving the barefoot Dandelion to commune further with the dolphin.

Now I know what I'm looking for. If Astrath has done the business with the gold in the statue he might be able to tell me where to search. He's already waiting for me in a landus at the corner of Quintessence Street and Moon and Stars Avenue. Gurd is there too.

'Any luck?'

'Yes. Ixial the Seer's aura is all over the gold. I scanned the city and found him in Twelve Seas.'

'Twelve Seas? You sure?'

'Yes. He's at the official residence of Prefect Tholius.'

Prefect Tholius. That's probably something that's going to make sense when I have time to think about it.

'What are you going to do?' says the Sorcerer.

'Find the healing stone. Kill anyone who gets in my way.'

'Lets go,' says Gurd.

His axe hangs at his hip. It's good to have Gurd along. It's a long time since we fought anyone together. I tell Astrath he doesn't need to come too. If he gets involved in a brawl with Prefect Tholius he'll never be readmitted to the Sorcerers Guild. But he wants to come anyway. There's no time to argue so we set off fast for Tholius's official residence in Tranquillity Lane which, apart from the church and the public baths, is the only decent building in Twelve Seas.

I'm trying to think of the best way to approach matters. I just don't have time for anything fancy. If I'm lucky Ixial will gladly hand over the dolphins' healing stone, but it's not too likely. For one thing he'll want to keep such a useful item for himself. For another, it would mean publicly admitting to theft from the dolphins. While that isn't actually a crime, it's a taboo act and would effectively end his career as head of a monastery.

I seethe with frustration as heavy traffic hinders our progress. We ride in silence, knowing that every second we are away Makri is very likely to die.

When we reach Tranquillity Lane and turn into the side street leading to the official residence we have a stroke of good fortune. Prefect Tholius himself is walking towards us in the company of Ixial the Seer. They're alone, without bodyguards, and they're taken by surprise as we screech to a halt and leap from the landus.

Suddenly confronted by an Investigator, a Barbarian and a Sorcerer, all apparently mad, the Prefect is taken aback. He demands to know what we want.

'The healing stone. And I want it now.'

'What are you talking about?' demands Tholius.

I ignore him and turn to Ixial. 'The healing stone.'

Gurd slips beside him and raises his axe. Ixial prepares to defend himself. I remember his reputation as a fighter. I don't have time for this.

'Kill them with the heart attack spell,' I say to Astrath Triple Moon.

Astrath raises an arm.

'Give him the healing stone!' yells Prefect Tholius, clutching nervously at his chest.

'He is not carrying a heart attack spell,' says Ixial calmly, proving that he can indeed see many things. He strides towards Astrath. I slug him hard on the back of the head as he passes by, and he falls to the ground unconscious.

'You didn't see that,' I mutter. I start to search him while Gurd keeps his axe close to the Prefect's neck.

'You know you're going to a prison ship?' rasps Tholius with impotent fury.

I find the healing stone. Small, black and shaped roughly like a cross.

'I'll see you on board,' I reply. 'Get in my way and I'll have to get you involved in the golden statue affair.'

Tholius's eyes widen and he suddenly finds he has nothing to say. I figured it was a safe bet he was involved somehow along with Ixial. It makes sense of his keenness to dispose of Grosex without answering too many questions. Makes sense of some other things, but I can think about that later.

We jump back into the landus. Gurd takes the reins and we set off. I pass the stone to Astrath and he studies it as we make all possible speed back to Quintessence Street. Dust floats up from the sun-baked earth and more pedestrians are forced to scatter as we pass.

'Worked it out yet?' I ask the Sorcerer. The Avenging Axe is now very close.

'I have never seen anything like it before. The dolphins say it fell from the sky?' He turns it over in his hands, studying it carefully. 'I don't really know what it is. It certainly feels powerful though.'

Darkness has fully descended as we arrive back at the Avenging Axe. I estimate I've been gone no more than an hour. I send up a quick prayer as I run with the others through to the back room where Makri still lies on the table with the terrible wound in her chest. Now gathered in the room are Chiaraxi, Tanrose, Dandelion, Soolanis, Palax and Kaby. Only Quen is absent. Misery pervades the scene.

'I've got the stone!'

I expect this to produce some signs of hope. No one shows any signs of hope.

'You're too late,' sighs Tanrose. 'Makri died.'

'No she didn't,' I protest. 'She just looks dead.'

She does indeed look very dead.

'She has a strong constitution,' I say. 'Elf blood. Orc blood. Human . . .'

Chiaraxi shakes her head.

Astrath Triple Moon places his hand on Makri's brow then takes out his lifestone and touches her skin. It doesn't glow, not even a flicker.

'Try the dolphins' stone,' I scream.

He places it first on her forehead and then on the wound. He touches it to the area just below her navel, where the centre of energy is located. Nothing happens, apart from Kaby expressing a great wail and slumping to the floor.

Astrath looks around helplessly. I grab the healing stone and try myself. Still nothing happens, though when I touch the stone I feel a warm glow in my fingers.

'It's not working. Piece of junk.'

Astrath, calmer than me, takes the stone back. Noticing that Dandelion's foot is still bleeding from the accident at the harbour, he bends down to touch the injury. Before our eyes it heals up wondrously. In a matter of seconds the blood stops flowing and the skin has regenerated itself.

So the stone does work. And Makri is still dead.

'Is she really?' says Tanrose.

'I'm afraid so,' replies Astrath, and Chiaraxi nods in agreement.

I take the healing stone again and place it on Makri's wound. Nothing happens. I stand there stupidly for a long time, waiting for her to come back to life. She doesn't. There doesn't seem to be anything else to do.

I take a tankard, walk through to the beer taps, fill it up, drain it, fill it up again, then walk back to where Makri lies and slump on the floor myself. No one speaks. The only sound is Kaby's sobbing, with a few others joining in as the mood takes them. Soolanis has drunk herself sober and sits rigidly in a chair with a bottle of klee, trying to get drunk again.

It flickers dimly in my mind that I now probably know most of what has been going on with the statue and Drantaax, but I'm in no mood to piece it all together. I have only two things in mind. One, I'm going to get drunk. Two, I'm going to kill Sarin the Merciless.

Heavy boots sound outside. Captain Rallee enters. If he's come to harass me about something he's picked a poor time. I stand up to confront him, ready to take out some of my anger.

He hasn't come to harass me. He's heard about Makri. Someone reported to the Guards that a strange young woman was shot down in Quintessence Street and he guessed the rest. He's come to pay his respects.

'I'm sorry about this,' says the Captain, looking sadly at Makri's body. Kaby is now crying uncontrollably. Without really registering the fact I notice that her boyfriend Palax's head is lolling on his shoulders and his eyes have the vacant look indicating a heavy dose of dwa.

'Who did it?'

'Sarin the Merciless.'

'What's behind it?'

'The King's gold,' I mumble, seeing no reason to conceal anything from Captain Rallee any longer.

I lead Captain Rallee through to the front of the tavern, now empty of customers. There I take the purse from my pocket and draw down its edges, exposing the statue underneath. The gold shines through, glinting in the light from the torches on the walls.

'That's the King's gold?' says Rallee.

I nod.

The front door opens.

'Correction. My gold.'

It's Ixial the Seer. He walks forward. Behind him the massed ranks of the monks of the Star Temple file into the tavern.

The upstairs door bangs open.

'The statue is mine,' says the Venerable Tresius, from the top of the stairs. He's slipped up the outside stairs and come into the tavern through my rooms. Behind him are gathered the massed ranks of the monks of the Cloud Temple.

The yellow monks descend the stairs in silence. The red monks fan out to meet them. Gurd, hearing the conversation, arrives to see what's happening. Captain Rallee looks questioningly at me.

The front door slams open to a heavy kick. Standing there is the bulky figure of Tholius, Prefect of Twelve Seas. He strides in with a great gang of armed men. Some of them I recognise as Civil Guards, though none are in uniform. Tholius is not wearing his Prefect's yellow-edged toga. I guess this is not an official visit. He's come to take the gold and kill any witnesses to his involvement.

Tholius surveys the scene briefly.

'Everyone out,' he orders.

No one leaves. His men takes their weapons from

their scabbards. Ixial the Seer studies the Prefect, as if trying to judge whether they're still partners. I could tell him the answer. A man who feels no qualms about robbing the poor of Twelve Seas is not going to share a golden statue with a monk.

There's a commotion outside and yet more people force their way in. A very tough-looking group of people, led by Casax. He's brought his strongest fighters from Twelve Seas and from the looks of the rest I'd say they've recruited from the gang lords of the surrounding areas. I'm puzzled why. If he's finally tracked Quen to the Avenging Axe he hardly needs an army to recover her.

Casax is briefly surprised at the sight of the Star Temple, the Cloud Temple, Prefect Tholius and Captain Rallee, but he adapts quickly. He laughs, in fact.

'I've come to pick up a little stolen gold,' he announces to the multitude. 'I see I'm not the first. Well, I'd advise you all to leave before you get hurt.' He looks pointedly at Prefect Tholius. As the government's representative Tholius should be in charge here but in practice the Brotherhood boss has more power. Tholius is well supported in the bar, though, and he shows no inclination to leave. Neither do the monks.

Casax turns to me, and grins. 'We've been looking for that gold ever since it was stolen. We had word the monks had something to do with it. And we had word you've been meeting with some monks, Thraxas.'

He looks at me sharply. 'You should know you can't hide anything that goes on in Twelve Seas from me.

I guess we'd have got here quicker if you didn't have that bafflement spell to hide Quen.'

'Have you taken her?' I demand.

'Taken her? What for? Quen works for me, fat man. And very clever she is too. We figured you'd lead us to the gold. As soon as she saw you showing off the statue she came back and reported it.'

Casax doesn't have to brag about it, but he likes to let people know when he's outsmarted them. Just another of his character traits.

'I hear the Orc girl's dead,' adds Casax. 'Sorry about that. Nothing to do with me. Anyway, if you'd all like to step aside while my men get hold of that statue.'

Captain Rallee strides in front of the Brotherhood boss. 'What makes you think you're taking the statue, Casax? I represent the law here, and I'll arrest any man who tries to remove it.'

Casax guffaws with laughter at the thought of a Civil Guard Captain getting in the way of a Brotherhood boss, particularly a Brotherhood boss with a full array of fighters in tow. They all laugh. The laughter grates on my nerves. With Makri lying dead next door I don't want to hear anyone laughing right now. I stand next to the Captain. I'd planned to kill Sarin but going down fighting these scum doesn't seem too bad an alternative right now. I feel like killing someone, and I'm not too particular.

'Come and get the statue,' I say, motioning to where it stands, half in and half out of the magic purse.

Everyone in the room waits to see who's going to make the first move. At this moment Soolanis lurches through from the back. Oblivious to everything and everyone around her, she navigates her way behind the bar, takes a bottle of klee from the shelf, and lurches off again. You have to admire the woman's single-mindedness.

Captain Rallee again demands that everyone depart and let the law take over. At this Prefect Tholius advances towards him and angrily demands that the Captain stop interfering. 'Twelve Seas is under my jurisdiction.'

'So it is. But I work for the Abode of Justice and a Guard Captain has a responsibility to uphold the law in every part of the city. Are you here on official business? If so, why are your men out of uniform?'

Rallee turns to Tresius who's waiting quietly at the foot of the stairs. 'And what do you want?'

The Venerable Tresius remains silent.

'They're all here for the statue, Captain,' I explain.

'Even Tholius?'

'In on it from the first. He provided Ixial the Seer with inside information about the gold shipment. And he provided Ixial with a nice house in Thamlin where he could meet Drantaax's wife and learn everything he needed to know from her.'

'Kill them,' grunts Tholius.

The place erupts.

CHAPTER
FIFTEEN

When I was nineteen I was expelled from the college for young Sorcerers. Having no money, no family and nothing better to do, I joined a company of mercenaries on their way to the war in the far southeast between the small city-states of Juval, Abelasi and Pargada. That was how I met Gurd, a large Barbarian of twenty-five or so who'd travelled down from the frozen north to see life in the civilised lands. That's what he said at the time anyway, though some years later he admitted to me that he'd actually been chased away by the outraged clan of a young woman he'd become rather too involved with.

Events in the south were confused, with the cities at war with one another. To make matters worse, each city had at least two claimants to the throne. On one occasion our company, in the employ of a Prince of Juval, ambushed some troops belonging to another Prince of Juval in the middle of a dense forest. At that very moment, the Army of the People's Democracy of Abelasi took us in the rear. While Gurd and I were still trying to work out which way our spears should be pointing, a joint force from the recently deposed King of Abelasi arrived along with his allies, the Pargadan

Army. No one knew what the hell was happening. In the dark tangled forest the companies of spearmen were soon splintered and disorganised, leaving a heaving mass of men struggling and fighting for their very lives with opponents they could barely make out. Panic set in as soldiers fought with enemies and allies alike in the confusion. There was nothing for me and Gurd to do, apart from hack our way through anyone and anything who stood in our way and hope that some time or other we'd arrive at an empty space where we could gather our wits, find a couple of horses, and get the hell out of there. Which we did, eventually.

I'm reminded of this day twenty-four years later as battle is joined in the Avenging Axe. Everyone wants the statue but only the last man left standing is going to carry it away. The monks of the Cloud Temple and the monks of the Star Temple lay into each other furiously, their lust for the gold fuelled by their bitter rivalry. The Brotherhood, enraged that anyone could even consider pulling off a criminal coup in their part of town, throw themselves into the fray. The gang members are not trained warriors like the monks but many of them served in the Army and they're all very experienced at the art of close-range street fighting.

Prefect Tholius meanwhile urges his men on. The Prefect has the most to lose perhaps, as his position in town is fast becoming untenable. Once word gets out that he was an accomplice in the gold theft he'll be stripped of his office and on his way to a prison ship faster than he can blink. Prefects can get away with many things in Turai, but not stealing gold from the King. Surrounded by his personal bodyguard of off-duty Civil Guards, he mounts a violent attack, determined either to wipe out all witnesses to his crime or make off with the loot to some other nation where he can live in luxury beyond the reach of Turai's laws.

Myself, I'm just caught in the middle. I don't want the statue. I wanted to solve a murder, but since Makri's death that's slipped well down my list of priorities. At the thought of her corpse lying next door blood fury rises in me in a way I've not felt for a very long time. I'm pleased for the chance to vent my wrath on whoever comes near.

Captain Rallee, as the only official upholder of the law in the premises, finds himself hard-pressed. He fights at the shoulder of Gurd and me, with the half-exposed statue protecting our backs. A howling monk of the Star Temple falls before his blade. I see he hasn't lost any of his old fighting skill.

Four Brotherhood men burst through the melee and set upon us. I parry a thrust, stick my sword through my opponent's thigh then gut him as he stumbles. Gurd chops a man almost in half and Rallee skilfully deflects a strike before running his sword up his opponent's blade and into his chest. The fourth Brotherhood man backs off, and we find a brief moment of space inside the madness.

'Couldn't you have brought a company of Guards with you?' I snarl at Rallee.

'Just came to pay my respects,' he says. 'And I want a few words with you when this is all over. Who do you think you are, withholding evidence? That statue should have been turned over to the Guard.'

'I was just getting round to it,' I grunt, and then it's back to the fray. Gurd's furnishings suffer heavy damage as people pick up whatever is nearby to use as weapons. Torches, tankards, chair legs and whole benches fly everywhere. Tholius himself picks up a huge wooden table and flings it at us before urging his men on towards the statue. Captain Rallee goes down under the impact. Gurd hauls him to his feet while I hold off two opponents with my knife and my sword. Everything is confused. I lose sight of both my opponents as a gaggle of monks flies in between us, screaming and cursing as they kick and punch each other senseless. I notice a young monk deflecting a sword thrust with his bare hands before delivering a neck-breaking blow to a Brotherhood man before himself falling to a sword thrust from behind. His companion screams in fury and leaps high over the sword then smashes his foot into the killer's face with such violence that his neck snaps like a twig.

Ixial the Seer and the Venerable Tresius struggle to close with each other, but are prevented by the mass of struggling bodies between them. Finally Tresius, who's seventy if he's a day, takes a jump from a standing position that any young athlete would be proud of. He rises, somersaults in the air while flying half the length of the tavern, brushes aside a few adversaries on the way down and finally stands directly opposite Ixial, at which Ixial smashes Tresius in the face, or tries to, but Tresius glides out the way.

They then engage in spectacular combat, each master displaying to the full the fighting skills they've developed in a lifetime of study, but neither can get the upper hand.

Another table pounds down on top of us and this time it's my turn to get knocked to the floor. Gurd manages to deflect the thrust of a long spear just before it impales me. I leap up and set about defending myself, but the situation is fast becoming hopeless. There's only three of us and we are now beset by Tholius's men on one side and Casax's on the other while monks rage everywhere in between. All of us have taken wounds and the floor underneath us is slippery with blood. Bodies lie everywhere and we stumble over them as we're forced back against the huge lump of marble.

I remember that Astrath Triple Moon is still in the background somewhere and I wonder if he might be preparing some mighty spell to get us out of this. Probably not. I dragged him out of his house so quickly he didn't have time to place any spells in his memory. He'd need a grimoire to read in a new one. If he has any sense he'll have disappeared out the back door taking Soolanis and Dandelion with him. So we're relying on sword power only, and that's starting to flag. I'm using my blade to parry the opponents on my right, while desperately deflecting blows from the left with my knife. I hack down another of Tholius's men, but the next one presses in on me immediately. I can't keep this up for much longer.

'Face it, Thraxas, trying to fight with two blades

you're as much use as a eunuch in a brothel,' comes a voice in my ear.

I whirl round in astonishment. It's Makri, a sword in one hand and an axe in the other, and she's looking pretty damned healthy.

'What happened?'

'I got better.'

'Well, you took your time. You expect me to fight the whole of Turai on my own?'

Makri grins broadly and starts laying about her with her axe and sword. Her gladiator battle skills clear a space round us, which is just as well. When Gurd sees her he is so surprised he cracks his head on the raised front hoof of Saint Quatinius's horse and takes several seconds to recover.

'Makri,' he cries, clutching his head. 'You're alive!'

'Sure am,' she yells back, planting her sword precisely in the chest of a red-clad monk unwise enough to try and hit her with a quarter staff. Captain Rallee, Gurd and I are inspired by Makri's return. We bring the advancing horde in front of us to a halt and start pushing them back. Monks, gangsters and Guards fall before Makri's axe as she scythes them down like a demon from hell let loose in the world for the purpose of slaughtering humans.

I get the impression that her brush with death has not soothed her anger over the way the monk kicked her a while back. She fights with a savage fury never before seen in Turai. No wonder they used to throw dragons, tigers and whole squadrons of Orcs into the arena against her.

Fighting is intense all over the room as the monks struggle with each other. The Venerable Tresius and Ixial the Seer, evenly matched, have stopped trading blows and now circle each other watchfully. Finally Tholius steps between them, raising his hands and bellowing at the top of his voice. The Prefect, who is something of a demagogue and has plenty of experience in talking to howling mobs, manages to attract the attention of the people around him.

'Stop this useless fighting,' he roars. 'We are just making it easy for them.' He points to us. 'Remove them and we can then discuss the distribution of the gold in a sensible manner.'

The remaining monks disengage from each other and turn their heads to where we stand in front of the statue. The Brotherhood men look questioningly at Casax. He nods as if in agreement with Tholius. Everyone seems to think that the Prefect has the right idea. Now, rather than fighting one of many battles in the tavern, we are faced with the prospect of a concentrated attack from everybody.

The entire assembly fans out to encircle us and starts to advance. We don't have a chance. In the limited space even Makri's amazing skills cannot stand up against such a weight of numbers attacking from every direction. Some of the swiftest monks are already scaling the statue to attack us from behind. Others take the opportunity to fling small throwing stars at us before engaging with our swords. None of us is wearing armour and both myself and Makri find ourselves with painful wounds as stars strike and dig into our limbs.

It's time for some swift thinking. I can do that.

'The magic space,' I roar. 'Everybody in!'

I jump on the statue's plinth, knocking off a monk who's scrambling down from above. Gurd and Rallee look dubious, but as the great Human wave starts to break over us they leap up beside me. I take the edge of the purse in my hand and climb into the purple void.

'I don't like this at all,' says Gurd, as I draw the purse over our heads.

'I wanted to see what it was like in here,' says Makri.

And then we are fully enveloped in the magic space, a dimension quite different from our own, where odd things happen, strange creatures live and Humans are really not meant to visit.

We plummet down through the thick purple atmosphere. Wispy clouds laugh at us as we pass. We land gently on a green grassy plain. A huge blue sun burns high above. Beside us is the statue, in all its glory, undamaged by my blows with a sledgehammer. Sitting on the bronze horse next to Saint Quatinius is Hanama, Master Assassin.

'Welcome to the magic space,' she says.

'Hello, Hanama,' says Makri. 'What are you doing here?'

'I heard you were dead,' replies Hanama. 'I came to pay my respects but you turned out to be alive. Good. As things in the tavern seemed confused I slipped in here till it quietened down. I was not expecting you to join me.'

I glare at her suspiciously. It's a bit much, finding Hanama here before me. For all I know she might have been sitting in the magic space for days. I could've been carrying her round in my pocket.

'Came to pay your respects to Makri, did you? More like came looking for Ixial the Seer. I know you have a contract on him.'

'The Assassins Guild does not discuss its affairs with outsiders,' replies Hanama coolly.

She's a calm woman, Hanama. Difficult to rile. She's small, and very pale. Assassins often are. The only pale people in Turai, in fact, apart from some of our aristocratic ladies who make a point of staying out of the sun for reasons of fashion. Sitting on the horse, with her thin body and black cloak, she looks like a child at play. She certainly doesn't look dangerous, though she is number three in the Assassins Guild. This is the woman who's reputed to have killed a Senator, a Sorcerer and an Orc Lord in the same day.

I'm not at all pleased to encounter her again. I detest all Assassins for the cold-blooded killers they are. The fact that they continually escape the consequences of their murderous actions due to the patronage of Turai's rich politicians doesn't make it any better.

It was rash of her to enter the magic space, though. I wonder if she realises it's not an easy place to get out of.

'How are you alive, Makri?' asks Gurd, a question I was meaning to ask myself before I got distracted.

She shrugs. She just woke up with a stone on her chest and a crossbow bolt lying beside her. There isn't so much as a scar on her body. I remember I left the stone on her, which was just as well. It must have taken longer to work on her than it did on Ixial, which is not surprising I suppose, seeing as she was so far gone she didn't even register on Astrath's lifestone. Quite something, this mixture of blood, I muse. I'll never believe Makri's dead again unless I see her lowered into her grave, and maybe not even then.

'An amazing artefact, the dolphins' healing stone. I wonder if I have to give it back?'

'Of course you have to give it back. The dolphins hired you to work for them.'

'No fee was agreed. If they offer me fish I'm turning it down.'

Captain Rallee suggests that they might have some sunken treasure to pay me with although the general consensus is that the dolphins are lucky for Turai so I shouldn't even be thinking about trying to make money off them.

'And they healed me,' Makri points out. 'I feel great.'

'You'd probably have recovered anyway, with a good night's sleep.'

Makri inclines her head towards the heavens. 'Nice blue sun up there. Hey, it just went green. So what else happens in the magic space?'

The marble figure of Saint Quatinius suddenly swivels towards Hanama.

'Get off my horse,' he says.

'All sorts of thing happen,' I sigh. 'It's really not a good place to be.'

Even Hanama, trained in every form of conceal-ment, both physical and mental, can't hide her surprise at being ordered about by a statue. She leaps down nimbly from the marble horse and gazes up suspiciously at the saint. He's now gone quiet.

'Did he *really* speak?' demands Gurd, who's raised his axe nervously. As a Barbarian he has never been comfortable with any form of magic, and this is all very strange to him.

'Yes. All sorts of things speak here.'

We look around at the continually changing colours of the landscape.

'Is this where you go when you eat the mushrooms Palax collects in the woods?' asks Makri.

This passes me by completely. I don't know anything about the mushrooms Palax collects in the woods.

'Well, now we're here, what's the next move?' wonders Captain Rallee, a practical man and not one to stand around admiring the view.

'Incidentally, is the purse still visible in the outside world?'

'Yes.'

'And we're inside it?'

'Yes.'

'Then what if someone picks it up and throws it in the fire?'

'Who'd do that? It has a golden statue inside it.'

'Prefect Tholius might decide to forgo the golden statue if he can get rid of all the witnesses to his crimes.'

I admit this is a troubling thought.

'Can you get us out of here in a hurry?'

Before I can reply a large pig walks by on two legs. It greets us politely. Gurd grips his axe and the pig notices this with displeasure.

'Oh! Going to chop me up, eh? That's a Human for you, chop up a pig without giving it a second thought. How would you like it if you were just going about your daily business and someone came along and chopped you up and ate you?'

'The Human race has been given dominion over the beasts of the field,' says Saint Quatinius, from his horse.

'Well, not by me,' replies the pig, and they start arguing.

I'm still on a high at finding Makri is alive but when I reflect that I intended to spend the summer quietly sipping ale and resting in the shade, and instead I now find myself inside the magic space listening to a theological debate between a saint and a talking pig while outside half of Turai's killers are waiting for me with swords in their hands, I get a little depressed.

The pig disappears without warning as bodies start raining down from the sky. At first I think it's more magical creatures. As the crowd of bodies floats to the grass – now a bright shade of orange – I realise that Tholius, Casax and the monks have followed us into the magic space. The lust for gold has no boundaries. We raise our weapons wearily to do battle again.

CHAPTER
SIXTEEN

Our adversaries come to ground looking confused and disorientated but it doesn't take long to get their bearings as Tresius, Ixial, Casax and Tholius marshal them into order.

'Kill them!' roars Tholius again.

At that moment the ground cracks open at our feet and a river emerges in a torrent, separating us from our pursuers. By the time they collect their wits they're looking at us across fifty feet of swiftly flowing water. I laugh. A very satisfying turn of events. I saunter down to the water's edge.

'Hi, Tholius,' I call. 'Fancy a swim?'

Tholius is nonplussed. Ixial the Seer is untroubled.

'The river will not remain for long.'

'I wouldn't count on your powers of farseeing working in here, Ixial. The magic space is very distorting, even for a man like yourself. Congratulations on your recovery. Now your legs are better you'll be able to walk up to the scaffold. Incidentally, it was rash of you to follow us. Just shows you're far too keen on gold for your own good. Do any of you have any idea how to get out of the magic space?'

From the looks of uncertainty that flit over the

various faces on the other side of the river I can tell that is something they haven't considered. Our conversation is interrupted by a brief but heavy downpour of frogs.

'So, Tholius,' I shout, as the last frog hops merrily away. 'What's the plan?'

'Kill you,' he roars back.

'Not such a bad plan, perhaps. Depends on your point of view. Another alternative would be to turn yourselves over to Captain Rallee here, and face the consequences of your illegal actions.'

Tholius isn't so keen on this. He likes his own plan better. Despite their losses in the tavern, the Prefect and Casax still have plenty of armed men with them. So do Ixial the Seer and the Venerable Tresius, so they'll probably be able to carry out his wish if this river suddenly disappears. I maintain a confident front and continue to torment Tholius from the safety of our present position.

Captain Rallee scratches his head. It annoys me the way he doesn't have any grey in his hair. Mine is just as long but it is starting to look streaky. I still contend that my moustache is better than his and it always has been.

'Thraxas. Just in case we ever get out of this place alive. And just in case I don't throw you right in the slammer for having the King's gold in your possession, how about filling me in on some details? I only came to commiserate at the death of your friend. I wasn't prepared to meet half of the city's low-life and a bunch of mad monks fighting over stolen treasure else I'd have

brought some men with me. I take it this is all connected to Drantaax's murder?'

'It sure is. It's a complicated affair. I'll simplify it for
you. These two groups of monks are rivals. Ixial the
Seer is head of the Star Temple and Tresius is head of
the Cloud Temple. They fought, partly about religion
but mainly about who was to be number one chariot.
Living up in the mountains drives them mad, I reckon.
You remember how hot it was when we held off the
Niojans at the pass?'

'Never mind the Niojans at the pass. What happened with the monks?'

'They fought, mainly. And then they split in two.
Both temples found themselves missing a statue.
Which gave Ixial the Seer a very good idea. He'd steal
the new statue Drantaax was making for Turai to put
him one up on Tresius and probably make the Cloud
Temple monks return to the Star Temple. And then
Sarin the Merciless, who used to be Ixial's student in
the martial arts, came to Ixial with an even better
idea. She knew Prefect Tholius back when she was
bringing dwa into the city. He was taking a pay-off to
look the other way, which is standard behaviour for
officials in this city, yourself excepted of course.
Whether the idea was Tholius's or Sarin's I don't
know, but it occurred to one of them that the gold
shipments from the King's mines passed by not too far
from Ixial's monastery.

'These shipments are a well-kept secret. The routes
and timings are only ever discussed in magic-proof
rooms lined with Red Elvish Cloth, but Prefect Tholius

obviously has connections at the Palace and learned when the next one was due. He gave the details to Sarin, who passed them on to Ixial. So the Star Temple robbed the convoy, slaughtering the guards in the process.

'Then came their very good idea. Instead of disappearing into the hills with the gold where they'd have been tracked soon enough by Palace Sorcerers, they brought the gold straight to Turai and hid it inside the new statue. You realise how safe that was?'

'Yes,' says the Captain, who is a smart guy. 'No Sorcerer would check inside a statue of Saint Quatinius. It would be blasphemous.'

'Right. The plan was to leave it there till the statue was taken out to the shrine. When the heat died down Ixial would steal it from the shrine, cut it open and take out the loot. Once he put it back together he'd have a nice pile of gold as well as a new statue. I guess he wasn't too worried about blasphemy.

'Which is where things went wrong. The Venerable Tresius had a spy in the Star Temple and he discovered what was going on and ever since then he's been after the gold and the statue for himself. The Cloud Temple made a full-scale attack on the Star Temple during which Ixial was nearly killed. He had to come to the city to get healed. By now Tresius had learned the gold was in Turai and probably in Drantaax's statue. He arrived too late to intercept it so he hired me to find it. I didn't realise that Saint Quatinius was full of gold though I knew something strange was going on.'

I gaze over the river. The monks are looking back at

us. Do they believe they are furthering their religion with this behaviour? Probably, if Ixial and Tresius tell them they are. A flock of silver birds flies overhead, turning gold and then white in front of our eyes. Heavenly music floats down from the sky. Fluffy rabbits emerge to play around our feet. It's cutesy time in the magic space.

'What really went wrong for Ixial and Tholius was getting involved with Sarin the Merciless. As soon as the gold was inside the statue and Ixial was lying crippled in the mountains she decided that it would be much better if she didn't have to share it around too much.

'She's a clever woman, Sarin the Merciless. Totally heartless, but sharp as an Elf's ear nonetheless. She knew that Sorcerers from the Palace and the Abode of Justice were looking for the gold. Old Hasius the Brilliant himself had been down to Drantaax's house. She couldn't load the statue on a wagon and ride out of town. She'd have been spotted right away. So she hunted around for some way of getting the gold safely away. And she hit on the notion of a magic purse. Rare items indeed, but she knew where to find one, thanks to her dwa-dealing days. She remembered that old Thalius Green Eye, who wasn't much use for Sorcery any more, was taking dwa up to the Palace in a magic purse. So she went and killed him, and stole it. And then, I think, she stole the statue, leaving some yellow flower petals to put Investigators off the scent. The Cloud Temple wear yellow flowers for ceremonial reasons. I guess that was her idea of a joke.

'And then something unusual happened. Sarin must have some shred of humanity in her miserable being because when she heard Ixial was being brought to the city to die she went back to see him. Being his student for four years might have stirred some emotion in her breast. I saw her try to kill Tresius, so she must feel something for Ixial. Sarin doesn't normally kill for anyone else's benefit. So I figure she felt something for her old teacher. Not enough to prevent her robbing him though.'

'I suppose if Ixial was going to die she wasn't really robbing him, to be fair,' says Makri, interrupting.

I frown at her.

'All these logic and rhetoric classes are bad for you, Makri. You should stick to being savage. Sarin practically killed you a few hours ago. Anyway, she was too smart to carry the statue in the purse when she went to see Ixial. He is a seer and might have perceived she had the gold. So she left the purse with the two men she'd hired to help her get the statue into the purse, a job she couldn't manage on her own. You could pull the purse right down over it, but you'd still need help to tip the base up. She probably told her two accomplices to disappear for a day or two and then meet her.

'Unfortunately they washed up in the Avenging Axe, which wouldn't have been a bad place to lie low if one of them hadn't happened to be a man I put in prison a few years back who was still looking for revenge. They were killed in the fight, which only brought their deaths forward a few days, because

Sarin would certainly have disposed of them when she was done with them.

'That put me right in the centre of things. Once Sarin learned where the men had been killed she knew I was involved and figured I'd probably ended up with the purse. She's been after me ever since. So have the Star Temple. Whether Sarin told Ixial some tale to explain why I had the statue, or whether his powers led him to it, I don't know. Which brought the yellow monks down on my tail as well, when their spies told them what was going on.'

I look down at the rabbit nestling on my toes, then up at the great comet that is now shining in the sky.

'Yes, Captain, while the Civil Guard has floundered around helplessly with no idea where the gold was, and these people have been chasing around after it, I've recovered it for the King. So don't give me the outraged bit about withholding evidence. I've solved a case that was quite likely to get you busted down to Private when you made no progress with it.'

I notice Tholius from the corner of my eye. He seems to be getting closer. Much closer.

'Damn it. Why did no one tell me the river was drying up?'

'We were all fascinated by your explanation,' says Makri.

'This is no time for sarcasm.'

'No, I mean it, really. I love it when you work these things out.'

The river is now down to about ten feet wide and the monks are starting to wade over.

'Run,' says the Captain.

We run. The sun might be green but it doesn't prevent it from being as hot as Orcish hell in here. I'm soon sweating badly and panting for breath. If we can reach a forest of yellow trees we'll have some cover. I struggle to keep up with the pace. Abruptly the forest disappears. Just vanishes into thin air. Damn this magic space. I halt at the statue of Saint Quatinius.

'Attack the heretics!' I demand, pointing at the pursuing horde. The statue doesn't move. So much for that idea I reflect grimly, and carry on running.

A giant castle hoves into view in the distance.

'Make for the castle!' yells Captain Rallee.

We make for the castle. As we approach, it disappears.

'To hell with this,' says Makri, unsheathing her sword and turning to face her opponents. 'I'm not running any more.'

'Please, Makri, not now.'

Makri plants her feet firmly on the ground, her sword and her axe in her hands, waiting for our pursuers to reach us.

'Why can't you just run away like a normal person?' I demand

'It's dishonourable.'

'Well how much honour was there in the Orc slave pits, for God's sake?'

'Not much. But I'm not running any more. That's that.'

I sigh, and draw my sword. 'Well, I'm too beat to run any further anyway. I never figured I'd be making my death stand under a green sun.'

'It's turned purple.'

'Or a purple one.'

Unwilling to leave us to be hacked down alone, Captain Rallee and Gurd stop running and stand at our side.

'Getting too old to run,' says Gurd, with a grin, which makes me remember what a good, cheerful companion he was when we were mercenaries together.

'Me too,' I tell him. 'And too fat. Well, we've got out of worse scrapes than this.'

'Sure we have. Remember the Niojan riverboat that thought we were crocodiles?'

We bellow with laughter at the memory. I doubt we're fooling anyone. Tholius and the rest are now very close. Having combined forces and concentrated their attack I wouldn't think it'll take them too long to dispatch us. We have no cover at all and even Makri's remarkable fighting skills can't prevent the monks from encircling us and sticking us full of throwing stars. Makri is wearing only her chainmail bikini. None of us are wearing armour. We'll take plenty of them with us, but they'll win in the end.

The talking pig makes another appearance at our side. 'Attack the heretics,' I suggest, without much hope.

'Sorry, I'm on holiday,' says the pig, and vanishes.

'What a waste of time this place is,' I say, angrily. 'You think we might get a dragon flying down to protect us or something like that. But no, all we get is a pig that talks about theology and then goes on holiday.'

I stop speaking rubbish for a second. Something has just occurred to me.

'Makri, I just realised who really killed Drantaax.'

At that moment the Venerable Tresius lands in front of me, somehow deflects my sword with the flat of his hand, and kicks me several feet in the air. It hurts. I'm bracing myself for it to hurt more on the way down when a terrific gale whips me up and blows me into a tree that has appeared from nowhere. Trees sprout up everywhere and suddenly a storm of random acts of magic makes it impossible for anyone to come to blows with anyone else. Ferocious insects of weird colours appear to torment us while the wind blows great gusts of purple hailstones about our heads. I notice Hanama in an adjoining tree, calmly waiting. I wonder if Ixial knows there's a contract out on him.

Combat is reduced to farce by the intervening magical forces. The trees disappear but before anyone can think about fighting again a volcano begins to sprout from the ground.

Everyone starts to look nervous as we wonder whether the angry-looking volcano will vanish before it erupts. Smoke pours from the apex and lava is starting to trickle down its sides. The earth begins to shake.

Captain Rallee looks at the growing volcano, then at me.

'How do we get out of here?' he asks, a demand echoed by Prefect Tholius as the ground shakes and groans and lava begins to pour in torrents towards us. Casax is a fearless man and stands his ground, but his

Brotherhood enforcers are starting to look nervous.

'A good question. And one which Prefect Tholius should have thought of before following us in here. Escaping from the magic space is no easy matter. How about you?' I call over to Ixial the Seer. 'Any suggestions?'

The volcano starts to erupt.

'Get us out of here!' roars Tholius.

'Why should I? You'll only kill us when we're back in the tavern.'

I turn to Casax.

'Not much point taking us all back to Twelve Seas if the Brotherhood starts coming round giving me a hard time, is there?'

Casax, still without fear, ponders for a second or two, then shrugs his shoulders.

'Probably not, Investigator. But I'm not too mad at you for this. We want the gold and I'm not giving up on it, but if you get us out of here I'll forget that you've been holding out on us.'

Molten lava is now pouring from the volcano and rocks are starting to crash around our heads. Any second now there's going to be one almighty explosion and Thraxas, Private Investigator, will never be seen again in the state of Turai.

I call over to Tholius.

'How about you, Prefect? You willing to walk away from the Avenging Axe if I get us back?'

Tholius doesn't have as much backbone as Casax.

'Yes,' he screams. 'Get us out!'

'And as for you, Ixial and Tresius. You better just

promise in the name of Saint Quatinius not to harm us when we return.'

Ixial and Tresius nod. I catch a look in Rallee's eyes showing that he doesn't think much of all these vows. Neither do I, but I'll have to hope for the best. The volcano shows no sign of disappearing and you can die here the same as anywhere else. If I get us out of the magic space I'll have to take them all with me, though I'd be tempted to leave them if I could.

I turn to Makri.

'Where's Hanama?'

She doesn't know. The Assassin has slipped off somewhere. There is a deafening explosion as the top of the volcano blows off and rocks the size of houses start tumbling around us. Ash rains down from the sky. It's difficult to breathe.

'Get us out,' scream a dozen voices.

'Okay. Just let me get a sandwich.'

I dig around in my bag and bring out one of the sandwiches Tanrose made me for my day's investigation. After all the running around and fighting it's looking somewhat the worse for wear, but it would do for lunch if I was hungry.

Everyone stares at me incredulously.

'Thraxas, this is no time to be thinking about your stomach!' cries Captain Rallee furiously as the molten lava starts to singe our toes.

'He's mocking us!' snarls Tholius. 'I'll kill him before the volcano gets me!'

Remaining calm I remove the top layer from the sandwich, revealing some or Tanrose's home-cured meat. I scrape a few grains of salt off the meat. The volcano erupts even more violently than before. A six-foot wall of lava surges over the rim and races towards us. Young monks scream and fall to their knees in prayer.

I drop the salt on the ground. There's an even louder bang and the whole world shakes itself apart in a fantastic earthquake. Abruptly the earthquake halts, the air shimmers, and the magic space starts to melt away. We find ourselves deafened but otherwise healthy, back in the Avenging Axe. The volcano is gone. No pigs lecture us. Gurd looks at me wonderingly.

'How—?'

'Salt. Complete anathema to the magic space. Destroys it. A little trick I learned on my travels abroad. The magic purse is no more. Only foreign bodies like us and the statue could survive. Everybody all right?'

The monks start picking themselves off the ground, dazed from their experiences but relieved to be alive. No one is looking too comfortable. When you are one second away from death at the hands of a massive volcanic explosion and then the next second back in a tavern in Twelve Seas, it takes a little time to adjust.

Prefect Tholius is one of the first to get his wits back. He checks that his ally Casax is still in one piece. Then, seeing that he still has a number of men in good health, he turns and points at me.

'Kill that man,' he orders.

I'm getting sick of hearing that.

The monks hold back, unsure of whether to join in.

And at that moment, as Gurd, Makri, Rallee and myself are wearily raising our weapons and thinking that really there must be some easier way to make a living, almost everyone in the tavern collapses to the ground and lies unconscious on the floor.

Makri and I find ourselves staring stupidly at a mass of assorted monks and gangsters apparently all having an afternoon sleep. The only other person still standing is Casax.

'What happened?'

'Are we still in the magic space?' demands Makri.

'You are back in the Avenging Axe,' says Astrath Triple Moon, appearing from the top of the stairs. I notice he's helped himself to a flagon of ale.

'Well done, Thraxas. I was a bit worried when you all disappeared into the magic space. That's really not a place you should go. But I thought you'd probably emerge all right. Salt?'

I nod.

'I've been looking at your grimoire,' continues the Sorcerer. 'Rather out-of-date, but functional enough. I thought you might need a little help when you got back so I had the sleep spell in readiness.'

He looks at Makri. 'I see your spell protection charms are working well.'

Makri and I both wear spell protection charms round our necks. They're made out of Red Elvish Cloth, which is immensely powerful, woven in with copper beads and wires and treated by Astrath. We acquired them a couple of months ago, fortunately, because a spell protection charm is vital to a man in my line of work. After I pawned my last one I was left an easy target for any malicious Sorcerer who came my way. Spell protections are rare items, and very expensive, and only the city's most important officials such as the Consul are issued with them as a matter of right, which is why Captain Rallee now lies sleeping at my feet, along with Gurd and everyone else struck down by Astrath's spell.

'Poor Rallee. They ought to pay him better. Good thinking, Astrath.'

Casax, an important man in the underworld, also has a spell protection charm so he's still awake, but I can tell he's at a loss for what to do next. I suggest to him he should leave before I summon the Guards and they start rounding up everyone connected with the King's gold. The gangster's face remains impassive but for once he has to admit defeat. Faced with myself, Makri and Astrath Triple Moon, he can't get to the statue, and even though he has influence in this city he won't want to be connected with the gold theft. That would have repercussions too strong even for the Brotherhood to escape.

He turns and leaves without saying a word. Now we just have to decide what to do with everyone before they start waking up. Makri suggests killing the ring-leaders while they're still sleeping. I admit it as a possibility but wonder if there is some less drastic way to make ourselves safe.

There is the slightest of sounds behind us as Hanama emerges from behind the statue. She wears a plain black necklace, the standard spell protection charm of the important Assassin. This Assassin has a great capacity for disappearing and reappearing when you don't expect it.

'I'm glad you're still alive,' she says to Makri, calmly, and walks towards the door.

'Don't bother thanking me,' I call to her.

'What for? I knew how to get out of the magic space. I took the precaution of taking salt with me.'

Hanama appears to have been untroubled by the whole affair. She's cool in a crisis, I have to grant her that.

'Is that really the King's gold?' she says, pointing to the statue.

I look at the statue and nod.

'It is.'

'Well done,' says Hanama. 'Another crime solved by your powers of investigation.'

She disappears through the front door. I stare after her suspiciously.

'That was odd.'

'She paid you a compliment,' says Makri.

'That's what's odd. Why? The Assassins Guild doesn't waste its time on compliments. Well, never mind. What are we going to do now? We have about ten minutes until everyone wakes up. I really can't stand any more running around getting chased by everyone. I'm sick of it.'

I am heartily sick of the whole affair. I started off just wanting to clear poor Grosex. Look where it got me. Next time a Prefect insults me I should think twice about losing my temper. But I probably won't.

I have to do something quickly. Tholius will be down on me like a bad spell when he wakes up. We could be back where we started and now I've destroyed the magic space there's nowhere to hide.

'You could leave the tavern before they wake,' suggests Astrath Triple Moon. 'I could shelter you.'

I'm not so fond of this idea. I don't feel like hiding.

'I could put the sleep spell back in my mind and send them to sleep again when they wake.'

'True. But we'd be here all day. The Guards would probably like a long talk with some of these people. It's no use going to the harbour station though. Tholius is in charge there and they'd just throw us in the slammer and I doubt we'd ever get out. But we could try Captain Rallee's station. Once his men hear he's in trouble they'll come.'

'What about the statue?'

'Without the magic purse no one's going to be able to move it in a hurry.'

It means leaving the sleeping Gurd behind, but he'll be safe enough with Astrath watching over things. They're not after Gurd anyway. Makri and I make to leave. I get a strange feeling as I walk past the slumbering figure of Ixial the Seer. A very strange feeling. I bend down to examine him.

'He's dead.'

'Dead?'

A slim dart is buried in his chest, just deep enough to reach his heart. An Assassin's weapon. I shake my head.

'That's why Hanama asked us to look at the statue.'

You have to admire the woman's skill. In the brief seconds I was distracted she threw a dart into Ixial's chest, killing him casually in passing. And no one could say they witnessed the event.

'No one escapes the Assassins Guild,' I sigh. 'Come on, let's get the Guards.'

I know most of the Guards at the Captain's station though that doesn't mean I'm a frequent or welcome visitor. Captain Rallee bans them from giving me information. But when I march in and tell them that their Captain is at present lying asleep in the Avenging Axe, with the Brotherhood, Tholius and two temples' worth of warrior monks waiting to attack him, and, furthermore, the King's missing gold secreted nearby, the station empties quickly enough. I stop off on the way to send a message to Praetor Cicerius. If there's a reward paid out for the recovery of the gold I don't want my share shuffled aside for some grasping Civil Guard.

It takes twenty minutes to make the round trip. When we get back the tavern has emptied entirely of opponents.

Astrath looks abashed. 'Sorry, I didn't have another spell to stop them escaping.'

Captain Rallee is still yawning. He glares angrily at Astrath Triple Moon for sending him to sleep though he admits there was nothing else he could do in the circumstances.

'You ought to get a spell protection charm, Captain.'

'On my salary?'

He starts barking out orders, sending men to the Abode of Justice and the Palace with news of what's been going on.

'You think Prefect Tholius will stay and try and bluff it out with his connections?'

'Doubt it. He's blown it this time. His connections will never smooth over his stealing from the King. I expect he's packed a bag and fled the city by now. Same with the monks. Was the Brotherhood in on the theft?'

I shake my head. They were just trying to pick up whatever they could. There's probably no way of making anything stick to Casax, not with the amount of bribe money the Brotherhood can feed to a jury when it needs to. Anyway, I can't see any jury convicting him of pursuing an Investigator and a Guard Captain through the magic space with murderous intent. It was established long ago in Turanian legal circles that the city statutes do not apply to events in the magic space.

A couple of Guards are wrapping up Ixial's body prior to carting it away to the morgue. When he saw the dart in Ixial's heart Captain Rallee didn't have to be told what happened.

'Hanama? You see her do it?'

I shake my head. 'She's too smart for that.'

'I hate these killers,' mutters the Captain. 'I'd be happy to see them all swinging on the gallows.'

He knows there's no chance of that. The Assassins Guild has too much protection because the Senate finds them very useful at times. So, it's rumoured, does the King. Besides which, they rarely leave any evidence of their acts behind them. If the Guards ask a Sorcerer to examine the dart it'll turn out to have been painted with fragments of Red Elvish Cloth, or spell protected, or manipulated in some other way known only to the Assassins to make it untraceable. Trying to convict Hanama of killing Ixial would be like trying to catch the breeze.

Rallee accepts a beer from Gurd. It's against the rules for Guards to drink on duty, but they don't pay too much notice to this sort of rule. The Captain is very pleased to have recovered the gold, but I can tell he's not happy.

'I expect you'll be wasting no time in going to the courts and presenting evidence to get Grosex cleared of the murder?'

The captain hates it when I put one over on the Guard.

I finish off my own beer. 'I'm going up to see him right now.'

Soolanis and Dandelion appear with Palax and Kaby. They've been hiding in the caravan out the back. Captain Rallee stares at them perceptively.

'Keep taking dwa and it'll kill you,' he grunts.

'Or I will,' I add.

Soolanis was bad enough as a drunk. If she gets into dwa she might as well sell her father's villa and move on to the street right away. It'll save time. And it takes Palax and Kaby enough time and effort to earn money busking, so I don't understand why they then want to spend it on some useless drug. Nothing would surprise me about Dandelion. I take the healing stone and hand it to her, but even this brings little expression into her vacant eyes.

'Take this to the dolphins when you get your energy back.'

I ask Makri to come to the law courts with me.

'You think Sarin might still be around?'

I shake my head. Sarin will have learned by now that the gold statue is beyond her reach. She won't trouble us again.

'She might be looking for revenge now Ixial's been killed.'

'I doubt it. I don't think her loyalty to her old teacher would go that far. Sarin is focused on her own needs. Anyway, it wasn't our fault Ixial handed in his toga. It was Tresius who hired the Assassins Guild. You know, I'm not sure if Sarin enjoys anything except killing. Makes me wonder what she wants gold for anyway. Probably wouldn't know how to enjoy it if she got it. I'll still kill her the next time we meet.'

Makri intimates that Sarin won't need me to kill her if she meets her first. She goes upstairs to put on her tunic before hitting the streets.

'Nice shape,' says Captain Rallee when she's gone.

'I guess.'

'You guess? Twenty years ago you'd have been baying at the moon if she walked by in that bikini, Orc blood or not.'

'Twenty years ago I wasn't old, overweight and full of beer.'

I'm completely drained. Captain Rallee takes us up

to the law courts in a Guard landus. It's a silent journey in the early-morning light. I guess I should be
happy as a drunken mercenary after coming out on
top against formidable odds, but all I really want to do
is sleep.

CHAPTER
SEVENTEEN

We arrive at the law courts with an hour or so to spare before the final day of the case begins. The sun beats down. There hasn't been a breath of wind in the city for weeks. Stals flop lifelessly on the statues in the forum. Sweat runs down the inside of my tunic. I'm fed up with the heat. I'm fed up with being fed up with the heat. In his black uniform tunic, Rallee suffers as much as I do. I notice that the Guards and officials of the courts still treat him with respect. He might have been bounced out of the Palace by Rittius but they know the Captain is worth ten of him any day.

In the forum outside the courts people gather for the business of the day; everything from petty criminals heading for spells behind an oar to wealthy merchants from the Honourable Association of Merchants involved in complicated commercial law suits. There are even a couple of golden-haired and green-clad Elves, sitting beside the fountain with an advocate and his legal advisers, poring over some old scrolls.

'Got fleeced on a deal to ship a load of silver,' the Captain informs us. 'Why these Elves still expect Turanian merchants to be honest is beyond me.'

Makri hails them in the royal language as she passes. The Elves leap to their feet in alarm, assuming that some important Elf Lord has arrived unexpectedly in the city. When they realise who has greeted them they practically fall over in their confusion. Makri grins and strolls on.

'I really thought Grosex killed Drantaax,' says Captain Rallee as he leads us down to the cells below the courts. 'He's such a sad little guy I couldn't help feeling sorry for him, though not sorry enough to stop him from hanging. I have to hand it to you on this one, Thraxas.'

A sad little guy is a fair description of Grosex when we reach him. It's the last day of his trial and he knows he's going to be found guilty and hanged in short order. When we walk into his cell he's slumped on his bunk. His face lights up with hope when he sees me.

'Thraxas! I thought you'd given up on me.'

'I never give up on a client,' I tell him. 'And I don't often lose one either.'

I pause, looking awkwardly around the cell. It's completely bare. There's nothing to focus my eyes on except Grosex.

'Although technically speaking, you're not my client. Prefect Tholius dragged you off before you could pay me my retainer and we never did get round to formalising the deal. Which is unfortunate.'

'What do you mean?'

'If you were my client I might have to think some more about it. Because I'm pretty unlikely to turn over any client of mine to the courts. Goes against the grain. Even if my client turns out to be guilty, I'd rather send him out of the city on a fast horse than hand him over. But as you're not really my client, and you did in fact kill Drantaax . . .'

I hold out my hands, palm upwards.

A look of terror crosses Grosex's face. 'I didn't!'

I'm tired. I feel bad doing this. I want to get it over with quickly.

'Sorry, Grosex. I've been everywhere with this one. I've involved myself with killers, monks, the Brotherhood and Lord knows who else. Makri nearly got killed and plenty of others were. When you start playing around with so much illegal gold it spirals out of control. You should have stayed out of it. You were always going to end up way over your head.'

'Are you saying Grosex is guilty?' demands Captain Rallee.

'Yes, unfortunately. Drantaax knew nothing about the theft of the gold. There was no reason for him to. His business was doing well. He had no gambling debts or drink problems. That was just a story made up by Grosex to give the sculptor some motive for being involved. But it wasn't Drantaax who Ixial approached with the proposition for hiding the gold in the statue. It was Grosex.'

I stare at the apprentice. He stares back helplessly, like a rabbit.

'Why did you do it?'

Poor Grosex seems unable to speak. Makri and Captain Rallee look on with interest.

'I don't really care why you did it. Maybe you just wanted money. Drantaax didn't pay you much. I've seen the room in Twelve Seas where you lived. Maybe Calia encouraged you. You wouldn't be the first apprentice led down the garden path by the mistress of the house eager to get her husband out of the way. But if she was involved I doubt she wanted you to kill Drantaax.'

I turn to the Captain. 'She went on holiday with Drantaax.'

'What?'

'On holiday. When the gold was stolen. They were having a break from the heat in Ferias. But when Grosex arrived in my office he told me he and Drantaax had been working on the statue round the clock for days. While Drantaax was away Grosex did the business with the gold. I didn't add it up properly till we were in the magic space and something reminded me.'

I don't mention that it was the talking pig that reminded me.

'Like I say, Drantaax knew nothing about the gold. Grosex loaded it inside the statue when Drantaax was away. Ixial arranged it all with him. And when Sarin's men came to the workshop looking for it, Drantaax learned what was going on. He returned from an appointment early and interrupted them in the process of removing the statue. So Grosex killed him. Stuck his knife in him. Simple as that. Unluckily for Grosex, Calia arrived back and started screaming for the Guards before he could remove his knife. And then he realised that leaving a knife with his aura in it sticking in the body wasn't the brightest thing he could've done, so he fled. He didn't have the nerve to try and make it out the city gates, so he ended up at my office.

'Which is the only smart thing he did,' I add, glumly. 'I have a reputation in certain circles for getting men off in dubious circumstances.'

And that's about as much explaining as I want to do. I turn to go, but Captain Rallee grabs my tunic.

'You mean you started all this for no reason, Thraxas? Grosex stuck a knife in Drantaax? That's what the Guards have been saying all along.'

'Well, you've got to get one right sometime.'

'So thanks for dragging us all through the magic space and damn near getting us killed.'

'I recovered the gold, didn't I?'

Captain Rallee isn't too pleased at all this. 'I'll remember your words about sending your guilty clients on a fast horse out of town,' he says acidly. 'Try doing that again and I'll be down on you like a bad spell.'

I walk out quickly, not wanting to catch Grosex's eye. I'm so keen to get out of the building I'm practically running when I get to the exit. By the time Makri catches up I'm well on my way to the nearest tavern.

'Don't feel bad,' she says, and takes a beer to keep me company. 'It's not your fault your client turned out to be guilty.'

'It still makes me feel bad.'

'If he'd paid you a retainer, would you really have got him out the city?'

'Maybe. I never like turning a client in. Bad for business. But Grosex deserves it. It was pretty cold-blooded of him to murder Drantaax. The sculptor might not have paid him too well, but he didn't do anything to deserve being killed.'

I down my beer and order another. With the heat and the exhaustion and all my exertions leading to this sad denouement, I'm not in the best of moods. I'm annoyed at Grosex and I'm furious at myself for being taken in by his sad demeanour. I'm humiliated at the thought of Captain Rallee telling his cronies in the Guards that they were right all along and that old Thraxas must be losing his grip.

Furthermore Captain Rallee is now annoyed at me and he's in a position to make my life awkward. The Brotherhood are none too pleased with me either. They certainly suckered me with Quen. It was a smart move for Casax to put a spy on me. I imagine the Boar's Head just burned down by accident and Casax immediately saw his chance to get someone into the Avenging Axe. Quick thinking on his part. I could take it as a compliment that the moment he heard about the gold and the monks he reckoned that I might well be the man to find it. What I mainly feel is stupid for not suspecting anything. All that time the Brotherhood and their tame Sorcerer were wandering around pretending to be looking for Quen, they were really looking for the gold. Only the fact that Astrath had put a bafflement spell on the place kept them at bay, I suppose, till I took it into my head to expose the gold right under Quen's nose. That makes me feel annoyed at Makri. She offered Quen shelter when she pretended to be on the run. I'm about to vent some of my anger on her, when I remember I'm pleased she isn't dead. I probably should mention that.

'I'm pleased you're not dead,' I tell her.

'Thanks. You don't sound too pleased.'

'I am. But it was pretty dumb of you to bring a Brotherhood spy into the house.'

'I didn't know Quen was a spy.'

I inform Makri shortly that she's bound to get us into trouble if she insists on bringing in every waif who's looking for sanctuary.

'Not as much trouble as you taking on clients who are guilty of murder,' retorts Makri angrily. 'You didn't even have to take him on. You just got annoyed because Tholius offended your precious dignity.'

'My precious dignity? I'm fed up with your stupid fixation with your own honour. You could have got us killed in the magic space just because you refused to run away from overwhelming odds. Good fighters know when to retreat.'

'You don't have to tell me anything about good fighting,' says Makri. 'If I didn't spend half my life doing some good fighting at your side you'd be dead and buried by now.'

'Is that right?' I demand, banging my fist on the bar. 'You think just because you could beat a few Orc gladiators you're number one chariot? I was street fighting before you were born.'

Makri is now irate. The heat has affected her as well. Customers edge away from us, wondering if swords are going to be drawn.

'Then maybe at your age you should be thinking about retiring,' says Makri. 'Concentrate on your drinking.'

'Well, I like that. Next time someone fires a cross-bow bolt into you don't expect me to save your life.'

'If you hadn't bundled into me in the first place I'd have avoided it and there wouldn't have been any life-saving to do.'

Makri and I are now standing toe to toe, glaring into each other's eyes.

'Oh yes?' I roar. 'It wasn't me bundling into you that made you get hit. It was taking dwa that slowed down your reactions!'

'I have not been taking dwa!' shouts Makri.

'Oh no? I saw you stumble when we met in Quintessence Street. How much time did you spend in Kaby's caravan with Dandelion and Soolanis?'

Makri is livid. The drinkers who had edged away now clear a wide circle around us.

'You fat drunk!' she yells.

'Don't call me fat, you pointy-eared dwa addict!' I yell back.

'How dare you say that!'

'Did I hurt your feelings? Why don't you go and tell your friend Hanama about it? She's always looking for some information.'

For a second Makri looks as if she really is about to draw her sword. Instead she slams her leather tankard down on the bar so hard the handle snaps off, then storms out the tavern.

I yell some more abuse after her.

'Another beer,' I say to the barman. For an instant he looks like he's about to ask me to leave the tavern but on seeing my face he thinks better of it and brings me a drink.

I'm about as angry as a wounded dragon. I can't stand it that Grosex turned out to be guilty after I decided he wasn't. I feel a little better for having someone to yell at. I finish my beer and get another. After that I get another. Then I get bored with the company I'm in so I make with a few insults about lawyers and head east to the Kushni quarter where I get spectacularly drunk with three mercenaries from Misan and a professional dice player from the far west and manage to forget what it is I'm so mad about.

CHAPTER EIGHTEEN

I wake up under a bush. Some time during the night I've crawled into a small park and fallen asleep. At least I kept enough wits about me not to lie down in the gutter.

I stink of beer, sweat and various nameless things picked up from the streets. While I've been chasing monks around the city I've forgotten to wash. If I don't visit the Twelve Seas baths soon they'll be dragging me away as a health risk. A few beggars look at me vacantly as I haul myself to my feet. I quickly check my purse. It's still there. I bid them a cheery good morning and start walking back to Twelve Seas.

I'm feeling in reasonably good form, all things considered. No hangover. I've noticed before that a lesada leaf seems to keep them away for a few days. I ought to sail down south and bring back a shipload. Make my fortune with them in this city. I'm less unhappy with life. So Grosex is going to hang. Hardly my fault. And if the Guards and the Brotherhood are on my tail, then so be it. I've managed this far with precious few allies in Turai. I guess I can struggle on now.

So it's in fairly optimistic mood that I head back

towards the Avenging Axe. Nothing like a night getting disgustingly drunk with some mercenaries to clear the system. Their leader was the size of an ox and dumb as an Orc but he was liberal with his money and very willing to buy a man a beer once he learned I was an old soldier with plenty of fighting experience. I remember a joke one of the others told about two Niojan whores and an Elf Lord and laugh out loud.

I find myself passing through Pashish. When I turn into the Road of Angels, a narrow street with tall tenements on either side, I remember that this was the address where Tresius told me he was staying while in Turai. Hardly salubrious, but good enough for a monk I suppose. Up in the mountains they're used to worse.

I wonder if Tresius is still in the city, and whether or not I should call in. He does owe me money, now I think about it. I found the statue. Things didn't go the way he planned, but that's not my fault. I realise there's little chance of him actually paying me anything but it will give me the opportunity to let him know what I think of people who come and tell me lies. And then hire Assassins to mop up the mess.

The tenement is not as bad as many in Turai but, with its crumbling grey stone and shaky timbers bleached by the sun, it's not the sort of place I'd like to live. Children have scratched their names into the stone and the front door hangs loose. Like every other front door in Turai, it's painted white but from the look of the building I doubt it's brought the tenants much luck. I push it open. Inside the torches are out and the staircase is dark. I walk up. Tresius told me he was living at the top. When I get to the topmost landing, it's so dark I can't see a thing. I'm fumbling around for a door when I walk right into it. There's a curse as it swings open into someone inside, then the noise of a person falling heavily to the ground. I'm in through the door in an instant, my sword drawn. I recognised that curse.

Just inside, struggling to her feet, is Sarin the Merciless. I place my sword point at her throat as an encouragement for her to stay where she is. Light from the room beyond filters into the corridor, and I glare down at Sarin. She glowers back up at me. Out of the corner of my eye I see something yellow. I risk a glance. Looks like a bundle of cloth, half in and half out of the room.

'The Venerable Tresius, I presume?'

Sarin doesn't reply. I warn her not to move.

'I'll be pleased of the chance to stick this through your neck.'

'So why don't you?'

I don't know, really. I take another look at the yellow-clad body. 'The gold's long gone. Why did you kill him?'

'He hired the Assassins to kill Ixial.'

'So? What do you care?'

Sarin doesn't reply. If it was anyone else I'd understand readily enough. You can't let your teacher be killed and do nothing about it, not if you've spent years in the mountains under his tuition. I just never figured Sarin to have any emotion. Then again, she did go back to visit him when he was dying.

'So you've avenged Ixial. And yet you were quite prepared to cut him out of the deal with the gold. You were heading out of the city with it yourself.'

'Of course.'

'You really are as cold as an Orc's heart, Sarin.'

I wonder what to do. Good fortune has arranged things so that the woman I swore to kill only yesterday is at my mercy. I just blundered in and knocked her over. And she has apparently just murdered Tresius, my client. Not much of a client though. I don't feel too much like avenging Tresius. But there is the matter of Soolanis. I told her I'd track down the killer of her father.

'And here you are. I might not be able to prove to the Guards you killed Thalius but his daughter will probably be satisfied when I tell her the murderer is dead.'

I press the tip of my sword a little closer to her throat. Sarin gazes up at me with contempt. She seems incapable of showing fear. Maybe she's incapable of feeling it. It would seem so, for even though she's lying helpless on the ground, a fraction of an inch from death, she has no qualms about insulting me.

'Thraxas, you are a bungling fool. Why anyone would want you to investigate anything is beyond me. I didn't kill Thalius. Not that I wouldn't have had it been necessary. No one would miss him apart from that drink-sodden daughter of his. But there was no need to kill him. I merely stole his magic purse when he was unconscious with dwa. I knew where he kept it hidden and it was a simple matter. But since learning about the plans of the Star Temple, the Cloud Temple followed me around the city. I imagine that the Venerable Tresius killed Thalius Green Eye later the same night.'

'You expect me to believe that?'

'I don't care if you believe it or not. But if you take a look in his robe you'll find something interesting.'

I keep my sword at Sarin's throat. Again I wonder why this killer, in her plain man's tunic and cropped hair, wears so many earrings. It seems inappropriate somehow. I use my toe to prise the yellow robe away from Tresius's chest. A bag tumbles out, flat but long and curved to the shape of the monk's chest. I stretch down carefully and examine it. It's full of white powder.

'Dwa?'

'That's right. Didn't you notice your client was a dwa addict?'

'Not with the way he was leaping round and fighting, no.'

'Well, he was. Which is why Ixial took over the monastery and threw Tresius out. And why Tresius couldn't resist robbing old Thalius of his supply when he followed me there, killing him in the process.'

I stare down at Sarin. She's such a ruthless killer with such a total lack of remorse for her actions that it seems unlikely to me that she'd bother lying about them. But I don't like the ramifications of this at all. Yesterday I had three clients. Today one of them is going to be hanged and another of them turns out to have killed the third one's father. The curse of Thraxas. If word gets out, my business will suffer a hell of a slump. At least it throws some light on Sarin's actions.

'You knew Tresius had a load of dwa. Easy to sell. Make up for missing out on the gold. No doubt that's why you killed him, rather than to avenge Ixial.'

'The two things happily coincided.'

What a mess. Dwa, gold, warrior monks and Sarin the Merciless. I'll probably never sort it out entirely. Sarin is waiting for an opportunity to get out from under my sword but I'm careful not to give her one.

'You almost killed Makri.'

'The bolt was meant for you. It would have killed you if your personal protection charm hadn't deflected it.'

I don't tell her that I don't carry a personal protection charm and only avoided the bolt by luck. Sarin stares up from the ground at me defiantly. I think I catch a slight trace of mockery in her eyes. She knows I'm not going to kill her in cold blood. I can't. I'm sick of it all. I sheath my sword. Sarin springs nimbly to her feet.

'You are a fool,' she says.

'So I'm told.'

'If you get in my way again I'll kill you.'

'People often tell me that as well.'

'Is Makri dead?' asks Sarin.

'No.'

She might even be pleased to hear this. It's hard to tell. She picks up her crossbow. Then she picks up the dwa.

'Thanks to you, Investigator, I'm not going to be

rich on the King's gold. This'll do for now.'

I make no attempt to prevent her. She slips through the door and disappears.

I glance at Tresius's body. 'Did you really kill Thalius?' I demand, but there is of course no reply. 'It was a bad idea to hire the Assassins to kill Ixial,' I continue, talking to the corpse. 'It's always a bad idea to hire the Assassins. They kill your enemy but it never stops there. Someone is always left wanting revenge.'

A crossbow bolt is buried deep in his chest. Despite this his aged face is serene in death. I wonder if I should search the place. I decide not to. Let someone else sort it out.

My optimism has vanished. Dead Body Thraxas strikes again. It seems I can't move in this city without finding a corpse. It wouldn't be so bad if they weren't all people I was involved with in one way or another. Grosex will hang soon. Ixial and Tresius are dead. Tresius killed Soolanis's father, more likely than not. I sigh, and head on home. It's hot as Orcish hell. Why did anyone ever build a city here anyway? A beggar holds out a withered arm. I drop a small coin in it. I send an anonymous note at a Messengers Guild post, informing Captain Rallee about the whereabouts of Tresius's corpse

I probably should've killed Sarin when I had the chance. Now I'll run up against her in some other case and in all probability she'll put a crossbow bolt into my belly. I grin wryly. At least she still thinks I carry a personal protection charm. Everybody thinks that. After all, I am a sorcerous Investigator, or meant to be.

But I don't have the energy to carry that spell around in my mind all day any more.

I couldn't just kill her though. Not in cold blood, just sticking my sword through her throat. I've seen enough corpses these past few days.

I call in at the baths and clean myself up, then struggle past the building works in Quintessence Street. Stonemasons curse their apprentices as they strain to winch the heavy blocks up the scaffolding, and foremen yell angrily at carpenters and plumbers as they struggle with their work in the heat. It's a relief to get home.

Makri is cleaning the tables.

'Hey, Makri, did you hear the one about the Elf Lord and the two Niojan whores?'

Makri glares at me with loathing and stalks off angrily.

Damn. I'd forgotten about the argument. It comes back in a sudden rush. Did I really call her a pointy-eared dwa addict? I sigh. Now I won't even be able to have a beer in peace to get me over my woes.

Dandelion appears. The one person I don't want to see.

She smiles at me very sweetly and hands me a small purse made of cheap cloth. She's embroidered my name on it.

'It's from the dolphins,' she explains. 'Well, the purse is from me, but what's inside is from the dolphins. It's to say thank you for recovering their healing stone.'

I open the purse. Inside are five antique gold coins tarnished from a long spell under water and a small green jewel. I remove one of the coins. It's a King Ferzius. You don't see many of them round these days, particularly in Twelve Seas. It's worth about fifty gurans. Five of them. Two hundred and fifty gurans. That's a good rate of pay in my line of work. My standard retainer is only thirty. A jewel as well. I'll get it valued by Priso at the pawnbroker's.

'Thank the dolphins for me,' I tell Dandelion. 'Tell them it's a generous payment.'

'I knew you were the right man to help them,' says Dandelion. She witters on about how I have some star lines in sympathetic alignment with the dolphins. I'm too drained to insult her so I just take my leave politely and head upstairs to my room, where I sit at my desk and stare into space. I realise I'm hungry. I need some of Tanrose's stew. If I go downstairs Makri will probably skewer me with her mop. I think it's time for her rhetoric class. I decide to risk it.

Tanrose ladles me a goodly portion of stew and a plate of pancakes to mop it up, but she gives me a funny look when I'm picking out four or five pastries to finish the meal.

'Makri is upset.'

'I noticed.'

'Why did you accuse her of being a dwa addict?'

'I was in a bad mood.'

This seems to me like an entirely adequate explanation but Tanrose doesn't think so.

'No wonder she was insulted. And as for accusing her of passing information to the Assassins Guild! You know how loyal Makri is.'

I raise my hands helplessly. 'I didn't accuse her of passing on information. I merely insinuated it. It was in the heat of the moment. I'd just sent a client off to the gallows. What did she expect me to do – stand around cheering? Anyway, she insulted me plenty.'

'Well, you're all grown-up, Thraxas,' says Tanrose. 'And you know half the people in Turai. There's plenty of places you can go to forget your troubles. I figure you can stand a few insults. Makri's young and she's still a stranger and she has plenty of aggravation about her Orc blood. She probably relies on you.'

'Relies on me? What about all those rich ladies in the Association of Gentlewomen.'

'I doubt she could count them as friends.'

'Fine. So now I'm feeling guilty as well. What do you suggest I do?'

'Take her some flowers,' says Tanrose immediately.

I scoff at this. 'Tanrose, you place far too much belief in the healing power of a bunch of flowers. I admit that the last time Makri was upset it worked like a charm but that was strictly a one-off.'

I had accidentally put her to sleep with a spell causing her to collapse in front of an opponent and naturally a woman as keen on fighting as Makri was enormously upset by this. So I followed Tanrose's suggestion and, to my amazement, Makri, on receipt of one not very large bunch of flowers, threw her arms round me, burst into tears and ran out of the room, actions which Tanrose later interpreted as meaning everything was okay. But that was only because no one had ever given her flowers before. She's not dumb enough to fall for it twice.

'Try it,' says Tanrose.

I sigh. If Tanrose can't come up with anything better than that then the situation is probably hopeless.

Makri bursts through the front door.

'Great rhetoric class,' she exclaims to the cook, then sees me at the bar. She walks past muttering about needing to air the place to get rid of the bad smell.

'To hell with this,' I grunt, and storm out the front entrance, none too pleased at the task in front of me. Baxos the flower seller has plied his trade on the corner of Quintessence Street for thirty years without benefit of custom from me. When I rolled up a few months ago looking for flowers for Makri, it practically caused a riot. This time it's just as bad.

'Hey, Rox,' he calls over to the fish vendor. 'Thraxas is buying flowers again.'

'Still got his lady friend, has he?' yells back Rox, loud enough for the entire street to hear.

'That's the way to do it, Thraxas!' screams Birix, one of Twelve Seas' busiest prostitutes.

'He's a real gentleman!' screams her companion, to the amusement of the workers atop the nearest building, who start adding a few ripe comments of their own.

I hurry home. I know this isn't going to work again. I will have some harsh words for Tanrose when Makri tries to stuff the flowers down my throat. I storm into the Avenging Axe where Makri is telling Tanrose about her class. I ram the flowers into her hand without saying anything and march around the bar where I bang my fist on the counter and shout for a beer and a large glass of klee. As an apology I admit it lacks a certain grace.

Almost immediately I am tapped on the shoulder. It's Makri. She embraces me, bursts into tears, then runs out of the room. Remembering events last time I'm fairly sure this is a good sign, but I check with Tanrose just in case.

'Does that mean it's all right now?'

'Of course.'

It all seems very strange to me.

'You know, Tanrose, I find this very peculiar. What the hell is so great about a bunch of flowers?'

'Lots of things, if you spent a large chunk of your life in an Orcish gladiator slave pit. Not many flowers there, I imagine. Makri's probably never been given a present before.'

I suppose not.

'You think it would've worked with my wife?'

'It certainly wouldn't have hurt. Didn't you ever give her flowers?'

'Of course not. I didn't know I was supposed to. I wish I'd known you when I was younger, Tanrose. Might have made everything a lot easier.'

I take my beer and a fresh portion of stew and slump at my favourite table, wondering about the mysterious ways of women. I reckon it's not really my fault I was never any good with them. They never taught us anything about the subject at Sorcerer's school.

CHAPTER
NINETEEN

Things return to normal, which is to say it carries on being hot. The street outside is full of building workers and I abandon all thoughts of work for the rest of the summer. *The Renowned and Truthful Chronicle of All the World's Events* carries story after story about the affair of the gold-filled statue and I get treated generously enough in the coverage, which is always good for business.

I manage to grab a piece of the reward for the recovery of the King's gold, though it's far from my fair share. By the time the Guards, lawyers, Praetor's clerks and sundry other city officials have taken their cut, there's not much left for the man who actually located it. I have to make a strong plea to Deputy Consul Cicerius to get even that.

We're sitting in the back yard where Palax and Kaby are playing a flute and a mandolin. The tavern has now emptied of visitors. Dandelion has gone back to live on the beach and Soolanis has returned to Thamlin, drinking less and organising a rich persons' branch of the Association of Gentlewomen, according to Makri.

'Was it Ixial or Tresius who started the whole thing off?'

'I don't really know. Once it was all over it was hard
to say. Hard to say who did what, or who was worse.
When I started off as an Investigator I thought every
case would have a crime at the beginning and a solution at the end, but often it doesn't seem to be like that.
Just a bunch of people going around, all behaving
worse than each other, so in the end even they don't
know exactly who did what. Still, I'd say they all got
what was coming to them, especially Grosex.'

He was hanged last week. I didn't bother attending.
Calia is back in Pashish, missing Ixial more than
Drantaax, I expect. At least she has Drantaax's valu-
able statues to see her through her old age.

'You know, I didn't even get paid by any of these
people? Apart from the dolphins, of course. All that
chasing round in the magic space and risking death at
the hands of Sarin the Merciless for no remuneration.
I must be slipping. I'll never get out of Twelve Seas at
this rate.'

'This'll help,' says Makri, taking something out of
the purse round her neck. It's a golden finger. 'I broke
it off the statue when we came back from the magic
space,' she explains. 'I thought we were due some sort
of reward. I'll halve it with you.'

'Smart thinking.'

I look at the golden finger. Half of that will make a
nice packet of gurans. I'm not doing so badly really. A
few nice cases over the winter, maybe some lucrative
work from the Transport Guild or even the Honourable Association of Merchants, and I might yet make it
out of Twelve Seas. If summer here is hell, winter's not

much better. And in the Hot Rainy Season, which comes up in about a month, the streets turn to rivers and beggars drown in front of your eyes. I can hardly bear to think about it.

I don't have to think about it right now. I pick up a 'Happy Guildsman' jumbo-sized tankard of ale from the bar and lie back in the shade. Listening to Palax and Kaby playing music, I forget all about monks, killers and gangsters, and go to sleep.

THRAXAS

Martin Scott

In the magical city of Turai, murder, mayhem and ruthless criminal brotherhoods are rife. The only people more corrupt than the politicians are the Royal Family. And the weather is awful.

It's down these mean, muddy streets that Thraxas, ex-soldier, failed Sorcerer and epic drinker, ekes out a living as a Private Investigator.

But when Princess Du-Akai, third in line to the throne, asks him to investigate a very delicate matter, it seems that his luck is about to change. And it does. A few hours later, he's in jail accused of murder.

Thraxas is a new star of comic fantasy. A man of extraordinary courage, legendary strength and nerves of steel he isn't, but his unique charm and very well-hidden talents are destined to make him one of the best-loved characters in fantasy fiction.

THRAXAS AT THE RACES

Martin Scott

It hasn't been a good morning for Thraxas.
A vindictive judge has just fined him almost every
guran he has, and two old enemies have threatened
his life. To cap it all, the rainy season has started and
it's wetter than a mermaid's blanket in the
magical city of Turai.

What Thraxas desperately needs is a winner in the
big chariot race. And a job. Out of the blue, his old
army Commander turns up with the promise of both.
The racing tip sounds a bit dodgy, but the job looks
like a doddle – just locate some stolen property.

Trouble is, when he does, the Commander is there
too. Well, his corpse is. And someone is sorcerously
tampering with the evidence to put Thraxas in the
frame. It's time for some serious investigating
in the rain . . .

<u>WISH YOU WERE HERE</u>

Tom Holt

It was a busy day on Lake Chicopee. But it was a mixed bunch of sightseers and tourists that had the strange local residents rubbing their hands with delight.

There was Calvin Dieb, the lawyer setting up a property deal, who'd lost his car keys.

There was Linda Lachuk, the tabloid journalist who could smell that big, sensational story.

There was Janice DeWeese, who was just on a walking holiday but who longed for love.

And finally, but most promising of all, there was Wesley Higgins, the young man from Birmingham, England, who was there because he knew the legend of the ghost of Okeewana. All he had to do was immerse himself in the waters of the lake and he would find his heart's desire. Well, it seemed like a good idea at the time.

Welcome to Lake Chicopee!
Welcome to your Heart's Desire!
And enter the amazing world of Tom Holt's new comic masterpiece.

THE SORCERER'S APPENDIX

Andrew Harman

All is not well in the kingdom of Rhyngill.
Despite regular payment of tithes, including
PAYE (Pay As You Eat), the citizens are all
tired and underfed. Firkin, a lad who is definitely
alpha plus in the get-up-and-go department,
blames the king, and sets out to find an assassin
who will rid the kingdom of its ruler. But little
does he know that the real villain is someone
else entirely – or that the origins of his friends'
troubles involve lemmings, pigeons and heavy
earth-moving equipment.

It takes a pieman, a magician and a knight with
a North Country accent to help Firkin see the
error of his ways!